Homework Tonight

With Answers

5

Revised Edition

Neville Hopper

Nelson CENGAGE Learning

Australia • Brazil • Japan • Korea • Mexico • Singapore • Spain • United Kingdom • United States

Homework Tonight 5 Revised Edition

Text: Neville Hopper
Cover design: James Lowe
Text design: Modern Art Production
Illustrations: Brooke Lewis and Dennis Sorenson

Text © 2004 Neville Hopper
Illustrations © 2004 Cengage Learning Australia Pty Limited

Copyright Notice
This Work is copyright. No part of this Work may be reproduced, stored in a retrieval system, or transmitted in any form or by any means without prior written permission of the Publisher. Except as permitted under the Copyright Act 1968, for example any fair dealing for the purposes of private study, research, criticism or review, subject to certain limitations. These limitations include: Restricting the copying to a maximum of one chapter or 10% of this book, whichever is greater; Providing an appropriate notice and warning with the copies of the Work disseminated; Taking all reasonable steps to limit access to these copies to people authorised to receive these copies; Ensuring you hold the appropriate Licences issued by the Copyright Agency Limited ("CAL"), supply a remuneration notice to CAL and pay any required fees.

For product information and technology assistance,
in Australia call 1300 790 853;
in New Zealand call 0508 635 766

For permission to use material from this text or product, please email **aust.permissions@cengage.com**

ISBN 978 0 17 097357 1

Cengage Learning Australia
Level 7, 80 Dorcas Street
South Melbourne, Victoria Australia 3205

Cengage Learning New Zealand
Unit 4B Rosedale Office Park
331 Rosedale Road, Albany, North Shore NZ 0632

For learning solutions, visit **cengage.com.au**

Printed in China by C & C Offset Printing Co. Ltd
7 8 9 10 11 12 13 13 12 11 10 09

About this book

Homework Tonight is a series of seven books, each providing 32 units (weeks of work) for each year of Primary School.

Each unit comprises:
- A story which should be read silently and then perhaps orally before completing the associated questions.
- Spelling of words from the story as well as the grade/stage list found on page 72. Activities to recognise correct spelling are also included.
- Grammar and word usage excercises often related to the story.
- Maths Knowledge and Skills excercises reflecting the work done by children at this stage.
- Research activities linked with the sciences and human society curriculum.

The series is designed to be user-friendly to children, parents and teachers. Answers are provided, but usually the required response is obvious from the information supplied.

Homework Tonight provides an essential core of homework experiences. Extension can be achieved by adding more colour to the page, reading and researching more widely about a topic or doing additional maths exercises of the types suggested.

Spelling should be reviewed each night and committed to memory using the Look, Cover, Write and Check method. It is more important for your child to be able to recognise misspelt words and know how to find the correct spelling, than to be able to spell a list 100% correctly.

Homework Tonight also encourages good story writing. A story written by your child, based on the story provided in the unit, can be a very rewarding exercise.

The series encourages multiculturalism and recognises the place ethnic and indigenous communities have in our community life.

As you work through each unit with your child, you should encourage, help and praise their efforts. Make it a game: develop your child's natural desire to complete the work at a high standard.

Because of the comprehensive nature of the series, you will be able to gauge your child's progress readily. As each unit is completed, you will notice improvement and will also be aware of problems for possible discussion with your child's teacher.

Teachers

Homework Tonight is a series specially developed for the use of your pupils at home.

Each book provides revision and reinforcement for the groundwork you establish in the classroom throughout the year.

The series also takes the haphazardness out of homework, by making sure that (whatever other work you may set) for four nights of every school week there are regular assignments covering every subject in careful progression.

Perhaps most important of all, the series is designed to bring close cooperation in the learning process between parent and child – the ideal support for the work children do at school.

Program/Register

A description of activities for each subject area is provided so that the parent or teacher can quickly appreciate the range of materials included. Each double page is designed as a week's work and covers all the appropriate skills areas.

	Topic	Lesson	Page	Date
UNIT 1	Reading: Spelling: English: Maths K & S: 2D Shapes: Number: Research:	T/T: Narrative. Read 'My Little Sister' and complete the single word cloze exercises Write words in bold print from the story and add some of your own Group nouns from the word bank Complete the ten activities Match polygons with names and draw diagonals Complete the algorithms Identify the insects and complete the crossword	8 9	
UNIT 2	Reading: Spelling: English: Maths K & S: Numeration: Number: Research:	T/T: Observation. Read 'Brave Explorers' and select the best phrase to complete the story Write words in bold from the story and add some of your own Choose the best article for each word Complete the ten activities Complete patterns, numerals and place value activities Complete the algorithms Match community facilities with basic needs. Two activities using Data Banks A and B	10 11	
UNIT 3	Reading: Spelling: English: Maths K & S: Rounding: Number: Research:	T/T: Narrative. Read 'Spaceship Endeavour' and complete the story using the code. Answer question about intentions Write words in bold from story and add some of your own Choose the best pronouns to complete the story Complete the ten activities Round numbers to nearest thousands, hundreds, tens and units; Write temperatures Complete the algorithms Group problems relating to space travel	12 13	
UNIT 4	Reading: Spelling: English: Maths K & S: Time: Number: Research:	T/T: Factual Description. Read the railway timetable and answer the six questions Write words in bold from questions and add some of your own Proofreading: Identify and correct the errors in each sentence Complete the ten activities Identify various time sequences Complete the algorithms Library skills. Use headings and sub-headings to find page numbers	14 15	
UNIT 5	Reading: Spelling: English: Maths K & S: Position: Number: Research:	T/T: Information Report. Read 'Whale Watching'. Cross out the wrong word in each pair and complete the story. Answer the question about whale sightings Write words in bold from story and add some of your own Choose the best pronouns to show ownership Complete the ten activities Identify co-ordinates on a grid Complete the algorithms Label humpback whale and complete cloze activity about how whales communicate	16 17	
UNIT 6	Reading: Spelling: English: Maths K & S: Area: Number: Research:	T/T: Exposition. Read 'Sandals or Bare Feet?' and correct the spelling to complete the story. Answer the question about Othelarni's freedom Write words in bold from story and add some of your own Write the subjects for the sentences Complete the ten activities Count units on the irregular shape Complete the algorithms Shells. Complete the wonderword	18 19	
UNIT 7	Reading: Spelling: English: Maths K & S: Time: Number: Research:	T/T: Narrative. Read 'Hidden Treasure' and mark the statements true or false Write words in bold from story and add some of your own Complete sentences using best verb from the Word Bank Complete the ten activities Show time on analog clocks and measure interval between two times Complete the algorithms Label the **root systems** and complete the word cloze activity	20 21	

	Topic	Lesson	Page	Date
UNIT 8	Reading: Spelling: English: Maths K & S: Fractions: Number: Research:	T/T: Factual Recount. Read 'Smash-up Derbies' and choose correct answers Write words in bold from story and add some of your own Select the best adjective to complete each phrase Complete the ten activities Complete the table and compare various decimal fractions Complete the algorithms Car safety and road safety. Questions. Draw a bumper sticker	22 23	
UNIT 9	Reading: Spelling: English: Maths K & S: Distance: Number: Research:	T/T: Factual Description. Study the street map and answer the various questions Write words in bold from story and add some of your own Proofreading. Correct word usage and punctuation Complete the ten activities Add distances shown on map Complete the algorithms **New Zealand**. Complete the summary about New Zealand's features and label the map	24 25	
UNIT 10	Reading: Spelling: English: Maths K & S: 3D Space: Number: Research:	T/T: Explanation. Read 'What's in a Watery Name?' and select the best word in brackets to complete the story. Answer the question Write words in bold from story and add some of your own Select the best adverb from the Data Bank to complete the sentences Complete the ten activities Complete isometric drawing and visualise number of faces Complete the algorithms Label seas on world map and colour in all the water. Answer question	26 27	
UNIT 11	Reading: Spelling: English: Maths K & S: 2D Space: Number: Research:	T/T: Factual Recount. Read 'My Brother's Car' and complete the story using the code Write words in bold from story and add some of your own Add position words Complete the ten activities Complete the table of polygons Complete the algorithms Match **occupation** descriptions to people who do that work	28 29	
UNIT 12	Reading: Spelling: English: Maths K & S: Area: Number: Research:	T/T: Information Report. Read 'Butterflies' and select true statements Write words in bold from story and add some of your own Choose the best conjunction to join the events in these sentences Complete the ten activities Select the correct area to match the drawing Complete the algorithms Identify **butterfly** facts. Draw some wings.	30 31	
UNIT 13	Reading: Spelling: English: Maths K & S: Subtraction: Number: Research:	T/T: Factual Description. Study the Football Draw and answer the various questions Write words in bold from story and add some of your own Editing. Select the two errors in each line and write them correctly Complete the ten activities Complete missing numbers and use a distance sign to work various subtraction exercises Complete the algorithms Complete description of each game. Illustrate and name them	32 33	
UNIT 14	Reading: Spelling: English: Maths K & S: Volume: Number: Research:	T/T: Factual Recount. Read 'Bail Up' and select correct answers Write words in bold from story and add some of your own Use of hyphenated words Complete the ten activities Calculate the volume of rectangular prisms and use abbreviations Complete the algorithms Complete various labelling and sentence activities regarding **Bushrangers**	34 35	
UNIT 15	Reading: Spelling: English: Maths K & S: Temperature: Number: Research:	T/T: Factual Recount. Read 'Ben Hall' and underline the sentence which does not belong. Answer the questions Write words in bold from story and add some of your own Change words to plural Complete the ten activities Complete a graph of temperature readings Complete the algorithms Complete the word puzzle about **Burns and Burning**. Work the cloze exercise as well	36 37	

	Topic	Lesson	Page	Date
UNIT 16	Reading: Spelling: English: Maths K & S: Multiplication: Number: Research:	T/T: Factual Description. Look at the television guide and answer the questions Write words in bold from story and add some of your own Editing. Check for spelling errors and punctuation Complete the ten activities Read the problem, write the algorithm and provide the answer Complete the algorithms **Television**. Label the video camera and answer the questions	38 39	
UNIT 17	Reading: Spelling: English: Maths K & S: Mass: Number: Research:	T/T: Explanation. Read 'Greenhouse Effect' and mark statements 'true' or 'false' Write words in bold from story and add some of your own Use pronouns to complete the sentences Complete the ten activities Count the blocks to measure the mass Complete the algorithms Locate **countries on world map** which produce excess carbon dioxide	40 41	
UNIT 18	Reading: Spelling: English: Maths K & S: Time: Number: Research:	T/T: Procedure. Read 'Fire Safety' and decide which sentences express the main idea Write words from story and add some of your own Choose words from the word bank to complete sentences Complete the ten activities Write 24-hour time on analog clock faces Complete the algorithms Label diagram of light effects of the setting sun. Complete the passage	42 43	
UNIT 19	Reading: Spelling: English: Maths K & S: Number: Research:	T/T: Procedure. Study the instructions and write the method in the correct order. Answer the questions Write words in bold from story and add some of your own Editing. Make the appropriate corrections Complete the ten activities Complete the crossword Create your own **meal** from the ingredients supplied	44 45	
UNIT 20	Reading: Spelling: English: Maths K & S: Fractions: Number: Research:	T/T: Discussion. Read 'Get off the Phone!' and choose the best of three words in the brackets to complete the story. Answer the question Write words in bold from story and add some of your own Vocabulary: Male/Female Complete the ten activities Colour fraction parts of shapes and solve the fraction problems Complete the algorithms **Telecommunications**. Unjumble the words to complete sentences	46 47	
UNIT 21	Reading: Spelling: English: Maths K & S: Money: Number: Research:	T/T: Explanation. Read 'My Pony' and choose a similar word to the one in the brackets. Answer the question about brother/sister relationships Write words in bold from story and add some of your own Using colloquialisms Complete the ten activities Complete table of prices/profit and discounts Complete the algorithms Identify statements about various types of **horses**	48 49	
UNIT 22	Reading: Spelling: English: Maths K & S: Graphing: Number: Research:	T/T: Factual Description. Study the dictionary page and answer the questions Write words in bold from dictionary and add some of your own Add nouns to the word groups Complete the ten activities Graph times on a chart Complete the algorithms Label the map of **Tasmania** and complete the information boxes	50 51	
UNIT 23	Reading: Spelling: English: Maths K & S: 3D Space: Number: Research:	T/T: Observation. Read 'Bugbear' and decide if the statements are true or false Write words in bold from the story and add some of your own Add words to complete the analogies Complete the ten activities Complete the table of properties Complete the algorithms Complete the information about **computers**	52 53	

	Topic	Lesson	Page	Date
UNIT 24	Reading: Spelling: English: Maths K & S: Division: Number: Research:	T/T: Personal Response. Study the statements and decide if they are facts or opinions Write words in bold from the story and add some of your own Contents and containers Complete the ten activities Complete the examples, showing remainders Complete the algorithms Complete the **dinosaur** passage and put skin on the skeleton	54 55	
UNIT 25	Reading: Spelling: English: Maths K & S: Co-ordinates: Number: Research:	T/T: Procedural Recount. Read 'Bike Business' and find out-of-place sentences Write words in bold from the story and add some of your own Add 'self' or 'selves' to words Complete the ten activities Identify places at various co-ordinates Complete the algorithms Aboriginal Rock Art. Copy a piece of Aboriginal art and list implements and subjects used. List other forms of **S-E Asian/Pacific art**	56 57	
UNIT 26	Reading: Spelling: English: Maths K & S: Money: Number: Research:	T/T: Factual Description. Study the phone bill and answer the questions Write words in bold from the bill and add some of your own Identify the adjectives and write them in sentences Complete the ten activities Work the problems involving money Complete the algorithms **Library. Categorisation**	58 59	
UNIT 27	Reading: Spelling: English: Maths K & S: Mass: Number: Research:	T/T: Narrative Explanation. Read 'Four Eyes' and complete questions Write words in bold from the story and add some of your own Tense of verbs Complete the ten activities Complete the table of kilograms, grams and decimal notation Complete the algorithms Label **the eye** and answer the questions about ophthalmologists	60 61	
UNIT 28	Reading: Spelling: English: Maths K & S: Space: Number: Research:	T/T: Factual Description. Study 'Mosquito World' and answer the questions Write words in bold from the story and add some of your own Rewrite sentences with correct punctuation Complete the ten activities Draw a mirror image and rotate an image Complete the algorithms **The mosquito**	62 63	
UNIT 29	Reading: Spelling: English: Maths K & S: Area: Number: Research:	T/T: Factual Description. Read 'Happy Holidays' and answer the questions Write words in bold from the story and add some of your own Add predicates to the various subjects supplied Complete the ten activities Find area of rectangles by measuring Complete the algorithms **Library**. Use of time lines	64 65	
UNIT 30	Reading: Spelling: English: Maths K & S: Graphs: Number: Research:	T/T: Factual Description. Study the credit card account and answer the questions Write words in bold from the account and add some of your own Match adjectives with nouns Complete the ten activities Complete the picture graph Complete the algorithms Complete information about the **history of money**	66 67	
UNIT 31	Reading: Spelling: English: Maths K & S: Fractions: Number: Research:	T/T: Factual Description. Read 'Tangled Tales' and put stories into sequence Write words in bold from the narrative and add some of your own Use best verbs in each sentence Complete the ten activities Complete the fractions table Complete the algorithms Various activities about **thunder and lightning**, including drawing pictures	68 69	
UNIT 32	Reading: Spelling: English: Maths K & S: Calculator: Number: Research:	T/T: Information Report. Read about the 'Great North Walk' and complete questions Write words in bold from the story and add some of your own Proofreading. Find and correct misspelt words Complete the ten activities Use a calculator to complete the numeration activities Complete the algorithms Complete the **outdoor adventure** puzzle	70 71	

Unit 1 Homework Tonight 5   Text Type: Narrative

Reading – My Little Sister
Fill in the spaces with verbs from the Word Bank.

"I hope you 1. _____ you 2. _____ to look after Nikki, today," 3. _____ Mum from the **kitchen**. I was on my way out the back door, ready to **disappear** to the beach. I 4. _____ what could I have been thinking of! All day with my four-year-old sister. Oh no! The **problem** with Nikki was that she 5. _____ **constantly**. " 6. _____ me to the park. Take me to the shops. Take me to the beach." She 7. _____ a real **pain**!

The **phone** 8. _____ and it was Gavin. What a **delightful dream**! What a **stroke** of **incredible** luck! He 9. _____ me to go to the beach with him, while his mother and his little sister would look after Nikki at the **library** where she 10. _____ . I 11. _____ Nikki. She 12. _____ out her lip and 13. _____ at me. "I don't want to go", she said. "I 14. _____ Gavin's sister. She's too bossy. "Oh no! My great day was turning into a **disaster**."

Q: Why was my day turning into a disaster?
_____
_____

Word Bank
• nagged • Take • wanted • wondered
• worked • stuck • glared • called • could be
• rang • agreed • told • hate • remember

Spelling
Write six different words from this week's spelling list on page 72 then choose six interesting words in bold from this week's story that you'd like to learn to spell.

Class Spelling

Story Spelling

Spelling Activity: Circle the misspelt words from the story and the list and rewrite them correctly.

disappear   fone   disaster   kichen   battery   skipping   abord   litning

_____

English
Select the best noun from the data bank for each category.
(First letter of each word is provided).

1. Human   w _____
2. Non-human w _____
3. Concrete c _____
4. Abstract l _____
5. Specific t _____
6. Non-specific a _____

Word Bank
• woman • computer
• a table • love
• the road • wombat

8

Unit 1 Homework Tonight 5

Maths – Knowledge/Skills

1. 87 + 94 + 305 = _____
2. Double 17 _____
3. What shape is a tennis ball? _____
4. What is the value of 5 in 358? _____
5. 88 – 35 = _____
6. Draw the top view of this shoebox:
7. Draw a triangular prism:
8. 21 + 43 + 17 + 67 + 59 = _____
9. Write the largest number you can, using: 1, 5, 8 _____
10. Name this object: _____

Space and Geometry

2D Shapes

Match the polygons with their names, draw diagonals on each shape.

hexagon

trapezium

rhombus

octagon

Number

1. 3,567
   + 6,936

2. 190
   – 68

3. 457
   × 7

4. 3) 693

Research – Insects

Find the insect that best matches each sentence and fits the crossword.

Across

1. Eats wood: _____
2. Eats aphids: _____
3. A general name for a group of insects: _____

Down

4. Lays lots of eggs: _____
5. Bird-biting: _____
6. A busy worker: _____
7. Makes a chirping noise: _____

Select one insect and write the description from a dictionary.

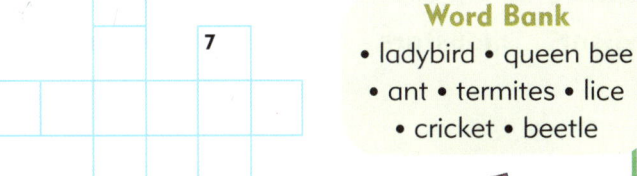

Word Bank
• ladybird • queen bee
• ant • termites • lice
• cricket • beetle

Child's Signature _____   9   Teacher's / Parent Signature _____

Unit 2 Homework Tonight 5   Text Type: Observation

Reading – Brave Explorers   Add phrases from the data bank.

1. _____ people living 2. _____ did not know what the rest of the world was like. Brave sailors made long **voyages** 3. _____ to discover new worlds and to draw maps of them. These voyages often took years to **complete** and many **sailors** died from accidents or disease.

Often explorers' ships ran aground 4. _____ or were broken up 5. _____ . They might be **blown** off course by **violent** winds or not be able to sail anywhere because the wind had dropped **completely**. A **fierce** storm might drive the ship 6. _____ while the crew struggled for control.

Early sailors were very frightened of unknown **dangers** 7. _____ . They feared **monsters**, **giants** and sea serpents. They imagined that a **sudden** whirlpool might suck their ship down 8. _____ .

Q: Write two real problems and two imaginary problems for sailors.
Real: _____
Imaginary: _____

Data Bank
• into the depths • on sandbanks
• Hundreds of years ago
• on sunken reefs • in tiny, frail ships • in strange lands
• in Europe • for days

Spelling
Write six different words from this week's spelling list on page 72 then choose six interesting words in bold from this week's story that you'd like to learn to spell.

Class Spelling		Story Spelling	

Spelling Activity: Circle the misspelt words from the story and the list and rewrite them correctly.

vilent   monstars   complete   giants   absence   beginer   giuide   electricity

English
Write articles 'a' or 'an' for these words.
(Words beginning with a vowel are preceded by "an".)

1. _____ apple   4. _____ tent   7. _____ fun-park   10. _____ surprise
2. _____ egg   5. _____ world   8. _____ giraffe   11. _____ elephant
3. _____ printer   6. _____ insect   9. _____ highway   12. _____ sentence

Unit 2 Homework Tonight 5

Maths – Knowledge/Skills

1. Days in March? _____
2. Write the factors of 16: _____
3. Name these shapes:
   a) _____ b) _____
4. Add these capacities:
   3L 120 mL + 2L 630 mL = _____
5. 231 – 4 = _____
6. 6L – 4L 500 mL = _____
7. What shape is the base of a cone?
   _____
8. Share $28 amongst 4 people.
   How much each? _____
9. Put these times on the clock faces:
   a) 12:27   b) 3:48
10. 48 months = _____ years

Numeration

Complete these patterns:
1. 3 6 12 ___ 48 ___
2. 640 320 160 ___ 40 ___ 5
3. $2\frac{1}{2}$ 5 $7\frac{1}{2}$ ___ $12\frac{1}{2}$ ___ ___ 20
4. A4 B8 C12 ___ ___ ___ H32

Write these numbers in numerals:
5. Eleven thousand, four hundred and twenty-two _____
6. Thirty-one thousand, three hundred and fifty-eight _____
7. Forty-three thousand and one _____
8. Twenty-two thousand, nine hundred and ninety-five _____

Identify the place value in bold in these numbers:
9. **3**4 579 _____   10. 5**6** 792 _____
11. 47 **9**01 _____   12. 21 3**9**0 _____

Number

1. 2,479
   + 4,696

2. 1,837
   – 477

3. 12.5
   × 7

4. 12.5
   67.4
   + 58.8

Research – Community

Match the community facilities in the data bank with the basic areas of needs listed below.

• Base Hospital • Telstra • Charlestown Buses • Fixem Medical Centre
• Jo's Suits • The Sports Centre • Guard Security • Bob's Bikes
• Police Station • Charlestown Square • Civic Theatre • Digital Phones

1. Protection and Security
   (i) _____ (ii) _____
2. Communication
   (i) _____ (ii) _____
3. Entertainment and Recreation
   (i) _____ (ii) _____
4. Retailing
   (i) _____ (ii) _____
5. Transport
   (i) _____ (ii) _____
6. Medical Facilities
   (i) _____ (ii) _____

If you lived in these communities, what would be your basic need? Refer to the Data Bank.
1. An oasis town in Egypt _____
2. A rainforest settlement _____
3. A village in Vietnam _____
4. A large city _____
5. A research base in the Antarctic _____

Data Bank
• carrying of fresh water • rainfall to help grow rice
• a means of shelter
• regular supply of services • warmth

Child's Signature _____   Teacher's / Parent Signature _____

Unit 3 Homework Tonight 5

Text Type: Narrative

Reading – Spaceship Endeavour (Use the code)

As the huge screen **1.** _containing_ **images** of the approaching spacecraft burst into life, you could feel the **tension**. Captain and crew alike were edgy as the impending collision drew nearer. Protection shields were in place but nonetheless, everyone was braced for a **2.** _disaster_.

Far out in space the **enormous** **3.** _structure_ named Spaceship Endeavour had run into trouble. Specialised **nuclear** fuel rods which provided power for the whole station and in **4.** _particular_ the protection shields had begun to dribble a strange amber liquid.

Energy levels had been slowly dropping until Spaceship Endeavour had only one **option**. Proceed to Earth for repairs as **5.** _carefully_ and quickly as possible.

In order to do this and actually arrive intact, the trip had to be done in **6.** _visual_ mode. Use of the hyper-drive **facility** would have allowed the ship to travel **invisibly** through time and greatly speed up the trip but it was **7.** _inoperable_ and out of the question. Unfortunately, the trip home is through **8.** _hostile_ **territory** and even as we speak the enemy spacecraft is bearing down for a strike. No communication is **received** and no sign of negotiation is **9.** _acknowledged_. Spaceship **Endeavour** seems doomed.

Q1: What were the intruder's intentions? _____

Q2: Circle the best theme for the story | trouble with amber liquid | troubles in space | users of hyper-drive

Code	1	2	3	4	5	6	7	8	9	10	11	12	13	14	15	16	17	18	19	20	21	22	23	24	25	26
	z	y	x	w	v	u	t	s	r	q	p	o	n	m	l	k	j	i	h	g	f	e	d	c	b	a

Spelling

Write six different words from this week's spelling list on page 72 then choose six interesting words in bold from this week's story that you'd like to learn to spell.

Class Spelling

Story Spelling

Spelling Activity: Circle the misspelt words from the story and the list and rewrite them correctly.

enormous   facillity   territory   opshion   employ   believe   produs   spaghetti

English – Pronouns

Choose the best pronouns from the word bank to complete the sentences.

1. We will see the movie _____ is showing tonight.
2. Will _____ please help _____?
3. _____ owns the new pencil case?
4. _____ saw the man _____ car was stolen.

Data Bank
- you • me • I • who
- that • whose

Unit 3 Homework Tonight 5

Maths – Knowledge/Skills

1. Write 57 in words: _____
2. Days in one ordinary year? _____
3. How many days between the 14th March and the 21st April inclusive? _____
4. Write as hundredths:
   a) 0.7= _____
   b) 3.69= _____
5. Read the temperature: _____
6. What is normal body temperature? _____
7. (23 + 46) – 25 = _____
8. 81 ÷ 9 = _____
9. How many days in a lunar month? _____
10. The pointed end of a cone is called an apex. True or False? _____

Number – Rounding Off

Write these numbers to the nearest:

	Thousand	Hundred	Ten	Unit
1. 1234				
2. 9862				
3. 6249				
4. 1045				

Temperatures: Write these in short form:

5. Thirty-seven degrees Celsius _____
6. Five degrees Celsius _____
7. Fifty degrees Celsius _____
8. Boiling point of water _____

Number

1. 34,567
   + 47,807

2. 89.3
   – 35.7

3. 45.4
   × 6

4. 9) 8,172

Research – Space

Problems encountered in **Space Exploration**. Study the Data Bank and list each item under Spacecraft, Flight Crew, Ground Control or Equipment.

Spacecraft _____

Flight Crew _____

Ground Control _____

Equipment _____

Data Bank
- being weightless in space
- electrical power breakdown
- controlling the spacecraft
- escaping Earth's atmosphere
- talking to the spacecraft
- re-entering Earth's atmosphere
- being confined to a small area
- communication equipment out of range

Child's Signature _____   Teacher's / Parent Signature _____

Unit 4 Homework Tonight 5   Text Type: Factual Description

Reading – Railway Timetable

Mondays to Fridays Train from:	am	am	am	am	am	am	AirC am MWH	am	am	am	am	am	am	am	am
Hometown	5:49	6:25	6:32	6:42	7:32	7:45			8:28	8:38		9:23		10:36		11:23
Victoria	5:51		6:34	6:44	7:34	7:47			8:30	8:40		9:25		10:37		11:25
Warwick	5:53			6:46		7:49				8:42		9:27				11:27
Hamblin	5:55	6:29	6:37	6:48	7:37	7:51			8:33	8:43		9:29		10:40		11:29
Borderfield arr	5:58	6:32	6:40	6:51	7:40	7:54			8:36	8:47		9:32		10:43		11:32
dep	5:59	6:33	6:41	6:52	7:41	7:55	8:14		8:37	8:48		9:33		10:44		11:33
Ayre	6 1			6:54		7:57				8:50		9:35				11:35
Kyle	6 4			6:57		8 0				8:53		9:38		10:52		11:38
Cannes	6 9	6:41	5:49	7 2	7:49	8 5			8:45	8:58		9:43				11:43
Cockletown	6:13			7 6		8 9				9 2		9:47				11:47
The Terrace	6:17			7:10		8:13				9 6		9:51				11:51
Bobs Plain	6:19			7:12		8:15				9 8		9:53		11:20		11:53
Frankston	6:24	6:50	6:58	7:17	7:58	8:20			8:54	9:13		9:58				11:58
Ascot	6:29		7 3	7:22		8:25				9:18		10:03				12:30
Down Creek	6:37		7:11	7:30		8:33				9:26		10:10		11:16		12:11
Massey	6:42	7 5	7:16	7:35	8:14	8:37			9:10	9:31		10:16		11:25		12:16
Watson Hall	6:48		7:22	7:41	8:20				9:16	9:37		10:23				12:23
West Watson	6:55		7:29	7:48						9:44		10:30		11:36		12:30
Wyoming arr	7 1		7:35	7:54	8:31		8:57		9:27	9:50		10:36		11:37		12:36
dep	7 2		7:36	7:55	8:32			8:47	9:28	9:51	9:55	10:37	10:55		11:55	12:37

Letitia, Terri and Dean live at Borderfield and need to catch the train to and from school at Watson Hall. During the **holidays** they also use the train to visit their **friends**. Complete these **activities**.

1. If the children catch the 8.37 a.m. train, what time would they arrive at Watson Hall? _____
2. How long would that trip take? _____
3. If Dean **missed** that train, what would be the next he could catch and how late for school would he be if school started at 9.25? (The school is beside the station.) _____
4. Why **couldn't** the children catch the **earlier**, air-**conditioned** train? _____
5. On the first Monday of the school holidays the children wanted to go to the beach at **Wyoming**. What train would they catch between 7.30 a.m. and 11.30 a.m. to have the **quickest** trip?

_____

6. Why is it **useful** to have a train **timetable**? _____

Spelling

Write six different words from this week's spelling list on page 72 then choose six interesting words in bold from this week's story that you'd like to learn to spell.

Class Spelling

Story Spelling

Spelling Activity: Circle the misspelt words from the story and the list and rewrite them correctly.

mised   quickest   holidys   earlier   boundery   machine   studant   crouch

English – Proofreading

Proofread these sentences, circle the errors, then write the corrections.

1. I carn't make sence of these book's.
2. Me friend Mikki says there to hard.
3. She doesn t now if she can does the work.
4. The excercises is harder then the puzzles.
5. I can do them puzzlers easy.

Unit 4 Homework Tonight 5

Maths – Knowledge/Skills

1. Write 14 479 in words: _____
2. Three score minus sixteen: _____
3. (3 × 8) + (4 × 7) = _____
4. 100 g of devon @ $6.00 kg? _____
5. Write forty-three thousand, eight hundred and seventy-one in numerals: _____
6. 3 × 5 × 5 = _____
7. Round 345 982 to the nearest thousand: _____
8. List prime numbers between 25 and 35: _____
9. What is the angle sum of a triangle? _____
10. Dad drove up the highway at an average speed of 90 km/h. How far will he travel in 4 hours at that speed? _____

Measurement – Time

Fill in the missing times in the sequence.

12.00; 12.15; _____ _____ 1.00; _____
_____ 1.45; _____ 2.30; _____
_____ 3.15; _____ _____ 4.15

Write these events in their time sequence: bursting into flower; dropping seeds; growing a strong stalk; putting out roots

_____
_____
_____
_____

Number

1. 45,786
   1,093
   + 14,907
   _____

2. 76.81
   − 3.24
   _____

3. 487
   × 7
   _____

4. 8) 960

Research – Library Skills

Using an index and sub-headings.

Using the information in the back of this fictitious book about animals, complete the following:

1. On what pages would you find information about:
   a) Pink Cockatoos _____
   b) Toothbill Bowerbirds _____
   c) Flying Foxes _____
   d) Asian Cats _____
   e) Saltwater Crocodiles _____

2. Write the topic on page:
   a) 128 _____
   b) 150 _____
   c) 30 _____

3. Identify the pages that might treat the topic **Edible Seafood**.
   _____

4. Explain why information about sulphur-crested cockatoos might take two pages and black pink cockatoos only tone page.
   _____

Blackfish	96, 208
Bluefins	102, 128
Bowerbirds	275, 282, 284-5
fawn-breasted	146
golden	146
toothbill	146
Catfish	30, 79
Cats	329
Asian	192, 291, 301
leopard	209
tiger	291, 292
Clownfish	73, 87
Cockatoos	255, 280, 301
black	170
pink	171
sulphur-crested	172, 173
Crayfish	218, 267
Crocodiles	3
giant	150
Johnston's	317
saltwater	151, 314
Dibblers	260
Earthworms	15, 263, 314
Foxes	21, 292
flying	53, 327

Child's Signature _____   Teacher's / Parent Signature _____

Unit 5 Homework Tonight 5   Text Type: Information Report

Reading – Whale Watching
Cross out the wrong word in each pair.

I like to **splash** in the 1. surf/snow on a hot summer's afternoon and I'm sure you 2. do/don't too. **Occasionally**, you might like to pit your body against the 3. snow/sea and even swim through waves. If you're really 4. good/bad I bet you could swim for 20 metres through the pounding breakers. Imagine doing it 5. four/for 2000 **kilometres**. Humpback whales do!

Every year around June and July, they 6. swim/walk up the east coast of **Australia** from the cold Antarctic Ocean to the special whale nursery in the Coral Sea. In these 7. colder/warmer waters they can feed and rear their young without having to fight the **freezing** waters and ice packs of their 8. southern/eastern home.

One of the fastest growing 9. cities/activities along the coast during these months is that of whale watching. Armed with a good pair of **binoculars**, a 10. warm/coloured jacket and lots of patience, you head for a good **vantage** point and wait. If you're lucky your wait will not be very 11. short/long before you see a spout of water and a dark grey shape **wallowing** through the sea. Usually there are two or three adult 12. whales/sharks and a couple of calves in the pod. Really lucky whale watchers actually get to 13. see/sea these **massive** creatures frolicking in the waves and actually jump 14. dark/clear of the water. Can you **imagine** it, not only can they swim 15. long/short distances, but with the mass of a semi-trailer, they can jump clear out of the water.

What show-offs… Still, if you were 16. one/three of the biggest **creatures** in the world you would want to show off too!

Q1: Why are there more whales being seen in recent years? _____

Q2: Circle the ideas which you would find in the story.

surf board riding   whale watching requires patience
whales care for their young   semi-trailers carry heavy loads

Spelling
Write six different words from this week's spelling list on page 72 then choose six interesting words in bold from this week's story that you'd like to learn to spell.

Class Spelling

Story Spelling

Spelling Activity: Circle the correct spelling for each pair of words and copy the correct word.

massive or massife   binocullars or binoculars   magasine or magazine   style or styl

English – Pronouns
Choose possessive pronouns from the word bank to show ownership or possession. Use all the words.

1. This drink is _____ .
2. These bikes are _____ .
3. My cat had _____ tablets.
4. That blanket is _____ .
5. Megan brought _____ bike.
6. The new videos are _____ .

Word Bank
- its • mine
- her • ours
- his • yours

Unit 5 Homework Tonight 5

Maths – Knowledge/Skills

1. 40 000 + 5000 + 800 + 40 + 1 = _____
2. Write 65 835 in expanded form:
   _____ + _____ + _____ + _____ + _____
3. Rearrange these numerals to form the largest number: 72968 _____
4. How many blocks in this object? _____ 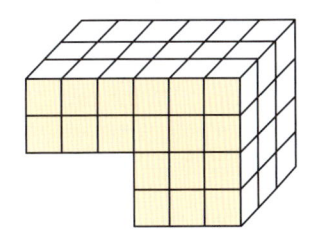
5. 2713 < 2731. True or False? _____
6. Find $\frac{1}{4}$ of 32: _____
7. Write the factors of 20: _____
8. Find the cost of 5 books at $2.85 each: _____
9. How many corners has a cube? _____
10. Write eighteen minutes past two in digital time: _____

Space and Geometry – Position

Write co-ordinates for each space marked on the grid.

1. _____ 4. _____ 7. _____
2. _____ 5. _____ 8. _____
3. _____ 6. _____ 9. _____

Number

1. 2,045
   2,361
   + 1,593
   _____

2. 2,406
   − 184
   _____

3. 49.7
   × 8
   _____

4. 5) 755

Research – The Whales

Data Bank
• baleen • flipper • blowhole • eye
• humped back • small back fin

Label features on this Humpback whale:  
1. _____
2. _____
3. _____
4. _____
5. _____
6. _____

How do whales communicate?
Complete this statement with words from the data bank: each beginning letter is provided.
Whales have no 1. v _____ cords, but force air past valves and 2. f _____ that are associated with the 3. b _____ and produce a range of 4. c _____, moans, whistles and even 5. s _____. Humans can hear some of these sounds, but others are so high 6. p _____ that only other 7. w _____ (or special instruments) can 8. h _____ them. Toothed whales read the sound 9. w _____ rebounding from 10. o _____ in much the same way bats do in flight.

Data Bank
• blowhole • objects
• vocal • flaps
• clicks • pitched
• whales • waves
• hear • songs

Child's Signature _____   Teacher's / Parent Signature _____

Unit 6 Homework Tonight 5   Text Type: Exposition

Reading – Sandals or Bare Feet?
Correct the spelling of each word in the brackets.

My name is Othelarni **1.** (witch _____) means 'he listens'. I'm 10 years old and I live on an **2.** (iland _____) in the Timor **3.** (See _____) with my family. Our house is right **4.** (besides _____) the water and I **usually** prefer to explore the beach than go to school. That's why I have a problem **deciding 5.** (weather _____) to wear **sandals** or to go barefooted.

If I go to school I must **6.** (ware _____) my sandals, but if I explore the beach, it's **7.** (diffrent _____). It's off with the **8.** (sandles _____) and along the beach, my feet **tingling** from the sand and **9.** (solt _____) water.

I've **10.** (decieded _____): No school today! No sandals either! What a **11.** (fealing _____) of **freedom** as I race along the beach. I'll **search** for shells or chase crabs. I'll dig my feet down deep into the soft, wet sand or run **12.** (thru _____) the incoming waves. Does this make you **13.** (envous _____)? Would you like to make a **14.** (desision _____) not to go to school? Well, don't worry. It's **15.** (Saterday _____) and you can come to the beach **16.** (to _____).

Q1: Why was Othelarni free to go to the beach? _____

_____

Q2: Which facts are true for this story?
☐ Love being bare-footed   ☐ school everyday
☐ sandals are never worn   ☐ sand is moist

Spelling
Write six different words from this week's spelling list on page 72 then choose six interesting words in bold from this week's story that you'd like to learn to spell.

Class Spelling

Story Spelling

Spelling Activity: Supply the missing letters to these words. Write them on the line.

sand__ls   se__rch   tin__ling   eno__mous   helic__pter   __unctual   suc__e__sful

English
All sentences have a subject. Read these sentences, then write the subject of each one.

1. Gum Tree English is very popular.

_____

2. Can I use the new computer tomorrow?

_____

3. The Australian Opals love their basketball.

_____

4. Does anyone have a spare computer disk?

_____

Unit 6 Homework Tonight 5

Maths – Knowledge/Skills

1. Write these numbers in descending order:
   18 563   9 572   14 925   94 735
   _____

2. (67 + 78) – 15 = _____

3. Write twelve thousand, four hundred and twenty-three in numerals: _____

4. Colour $\frac{1}{3}$ of the 15 blocks of chocolate.

5. Two years – how many months? _____

6. If Tuesday was the 10th April, write the date of the previous Friday. _____

7. $1 - \frac{43}{100} = \frac{}{100}$

8. Product of 6 and 9 = _____

9. Square 4: _____

10. Write 248 in words: _____

Measurement – Area

Find the area of these irregular shapes. Each square is $\frac{1}{4}$ cm^2.

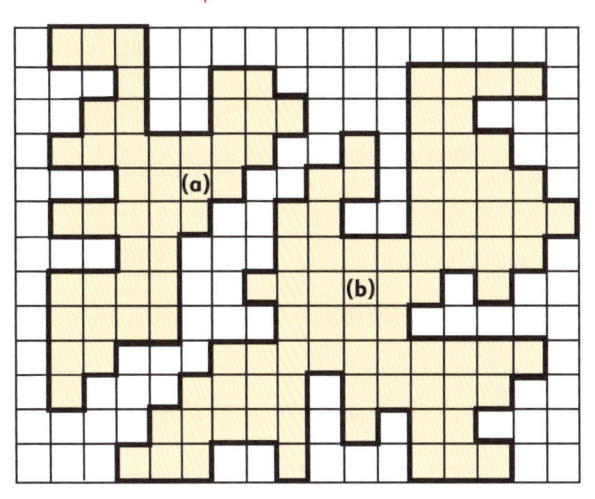

a) _____

b) _____

Number

1. 19,406
   + 23,609
   _____

2. 63,960
   – 45,958
   _____

3. 2,415
   × 5
   _____

4. 4)1,724

Research – Coastline

You would find a lot of these animals along the coastline.

Find the animals in the wonderword. Colour each one differently.

sea-urchin   periwinkle   cockle
pipi   sea-horse   rock-crab
bristleworm   sea-anemone

R	O	C	K	–	C	R	A	B	J	S
M	R	O	W	E	L	T	S	I	R	B
A	E	S	E	A	–	H	O	R	S	E
X	P	E	R	I	W	I	N	K	L	E
S	E	A	–	A	N	E	M	O	N	E
S	A	S	P	I	P	I	P	Y	N	M
S	E	A	–	U	R	C	H	I	N	L
R	C	M	A	B	E	L	K	C	O	C

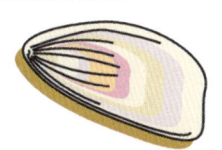

Place these animals in their correct group.

Shells   Active and Mobile   Attached to rock

Unit 7 Homework Tonight 5   Text Type: Narrative

Reading – Hidden Treasure

Read the story, then decide if the statements about it are true or false.

No sooner had Graham begun to cut into the root **system** of the camphor laurel tree with the **spluttering** old chain saw than he knew something was wrong. The saw hit something, made a high-pitched **squeal**, and stopped dead.

Graham looked closely at the **area** he had been cutting. He could see the **corner** of what appeared to be a **metal** box. Pulling and tugging, he was able to **wrench** it free. What could it be? Graham's hand shook a little as he opened the lid. His mouth dropped wide open as he saw that the box was filled with gold coins and jewellery. As his legs turned to jelly, he began to **wonder** if this was real or whether his **imagination** was working **overtime**.

T   F

1. Graham was cutting down a eucalyptus tree. ☐ ☐
2. Graham was using an old chain saw. ☐ ☐
3. The chain saw hit the metal box. ☐ ☐
4. Graham was afraid he'd broken the chain saw. ☐ ☐
5. Graham tried but couldn't free the box. ☐ ☐
6. The box was full of gold coins and jewellery. ☐ ☐
7. The box was empty after all. ☐ ☐
8. Graham was very excited by his find. ☐ ☐

Spelling

Write six different words from this week's spelling list on page 72 then choose six interesting words in bold from this week's story that you'd like to learn to spell.

Class Spelling

Story Spelling

Spelling Activity: Supply the missing letters to these words. Write them on the line.

w _ nde _   _ y _ tem   _ renc _   i _ aginat _ on   b _ si _ st

English – Verbs

Add the most appropriate verbs from the verb group to these sentences.

1. He _____ to his friend every day.
2. Dad went _____ the car with petrol.
3. _____ carefully is important.
4. I _____ very carefully in my book.
5. Mitzi _____ exciting books.
6. He had lots of bottles _____ .

Verb Group
• to think • to empty • wrote • to fill • writes • talks

20

Unit 7 Homework Tonight 5

Maths – Knowledge/Skills

1. What number is halfway between 140 and 180? _____
2. 160 + 287 = _____ + 160
3. Change 47/100 to a decimal: _____
4. Find the average of 3, 16 and 5: _____
5. How many school days in 5 weeks? _____
6. 30 years = _____ decades
7. Measure the diagonal of this page. _____
8. Measure the perimeter of a car number plate _____
9. $\frac{1}{4} < \frac{1}{8}$ True or False? _____
10. Write 1 285 in words: _____

Measurement – Time

Write the times on analog and digital clocks.

1. A quarter to three 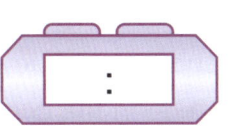
2. Twenty-two past eight 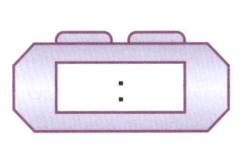
3. Fourteen minutes to ten

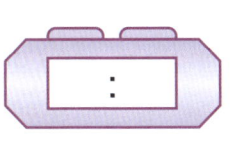

How many hours and minutes from the first time to the second?

4. 10.30 a.m. to 2.35 p.m. _____
5. 10.59 a.m. to 12.37 p.m. _____

Number

1. 13.67
   + 62.98
   _____

2. 237.60
   − 74.70
   _____

3. 45.9
   × 7
   _____

4. 5)1,590

Research – Plants

Select the correct answers from the data bank.

Try this experiment to discover how important 1. _____ are for normal plant growth. You will need 2. _____ or lids, some cotton wool, seeds such as wheat or brown rice, water and 3. _____.

1. Place a layer of 4. _____ on each saucer or lid.
2. Sprinkle the 5. _____ over the cotton wool.
3. 6. _____ one and place it in a warm sunny position to act as a control.
4. Leave another 7. _____ and place it in a warm sunny position.
5. Moisten the third and place it in a 8. _____. (No light or heat).
6. Moisten the fourth with boiled water and 9. _____ to allow for no air.

Data Bank
- four saucers
- Moisten • air, warmth, water and light • dry
- cotton wool
- seeds • cooking oil
- cover the seeds with cooking oil
- refrigerator

Write your results after two weeks.

Child's Signature _____ 21 Teacher's / Parent Signature _____

Unit 8 Homework Tonight 5   Text Type: Factual Recount

Reading – Smash-up Derbies
Read the story, then choose the correct answers.

Have you been to the motordrome? Or seen 'smash-up derbies' on TV? Watching cars drive as close as **possible** to each other is thrilling entertainment. The action is fast and **furious**.

Once a friend of mine, Jay, won a **raffle** which had an unusual first prize. The winner was invited to ride in the car with a smash-up derby driver. Amazingly, this was to be in an **actual** race. I couldn't **believe** that they would offer such a prize. Jay was allowed to take a friend along to the pits as he suited up for the big ride. The car was larger than the usual one and even had a special, fully **enclosed** seat provided.

Jay quickly donned the fireproof suit and was **strapped** in. Smash-up derby cars need to be at **peak performance** when they stand on the starting grid. Part of that preparation is to have the wheels steaming hot. Jay's driver knew all the tricks in the book and before I could blink, the amber lights were flashing, the green light snapped on and Jay was off in a **cloud** of dust and **petrol fumes**.

1. Jay's prize in the raffle was
   a) to drive a smash-up derby car
   b) to ride in a smash-up derby
   c) a smash-up derby car

2. The car Jay rode in
   a) was bigger than the usual one
   b) was smaller that the usual one
   c) was just the same as the usual one

3. Jay had to wear
   a) an enclosed suit
   b) dark glasses
   c) a fireproof suit

4. At the starting grid
   a) green lights flashed
   b) the cars' wheels are steaming hot
   c) the cars are close to each other

Spelling
Write six different words from this week's spelling list on page 72 then choose six interesting words in bold from this week's story that you'd like to learn to spell.

Class Spelling

Story Spelling

Spelling Activity: Circle the misspelt words and write them correctly.

furius   believe   performance   petrol   capetal   histery   pyjamas   suround

English
Add the most suitable adjectives from the data bank.

1. A _____ insect.
2. A _____ marigold.
3. Our phone's _____ .
4. My sausage sandwich is very _____ .
5. Her books are _____ .
6. Tye's _____ radio really works.
7. The ice is _____ cold.

Data Bank
- small • spicy
- white • freezing
- yellow • miniature
- interesting

Unit 8 Homework Tonight 5

Maths – Knowledge/Skills

1. Write 562 in expanded notation: _____

2. Add: 4L + 2L 563 mL + 2L + 330 mL = _____

3. Complete the drawing of a hexagonal prism:

4. 500 g of tomatoes @ $4.60/kg= _____

5. Value of the 8 in 4 892: _____

6. How many halves in $11\frac{1}{2}$? _____

7. 240 minutes = _____ hours

8. Write 2.835L in litres and millilitres:

9. Sum of 12c, 5c, 4c and 18c = _____

10. Write the smallest number you can, using the digits 7, 4, 9 _____

Number

Fractions and Decimals

Complete the table of equal fractions.

1. Out of 100				75
2. Decimal	0.45			
3. Fraction		$\frac{67}{100}$		
4. Percentage			39%	

Comparing decimals:

Circle the larger of the pairs of fractions:

5. a) (0.56/0.46)   b) (0.73/0.46)

Circle the smaller of the pairs of fractions:

6. a) (0.21/0.45)   b) (0.34/0.43)

Write the next higher decimal fraction:

7. a) (0.56, _____)   b) (0.35, _____)

Number

1. 89.56
   + 83.81
   _____

2. 569.28
   − 50.77
   _____

3. 68
   × 8
   _____

4. 7)258   r

Research – Car Safety

Discuss road safety, then tick the phrases that refer to positive aspects of car safety.

1. Leaving a safe distance between vehicles ☐
2. Lots of loose luggage ☐
3. One person per seat belt ☐
4. Watch the road ahead ☐
5. Ask the driver to look at objects away from the road ☐
6. Speed should match road conditions ☐
7. Speeding excessively can kill ☐
8. Drinking of alcohol by drivers must be limited. ☐

9. Tell why these points are important to consider: _____

10. What extra safety feature would you add to the list above?

11. Design a road safety bumper sticker.

Child's Signature _____   Teacher's / Parent Signature _____

Unit **9** Homework Tonight 5   Text Type: Factual Description

Reading – Street Map

Study this **street map** carefully, then complete the following **activities**.

1. Colour:
   - sports ground and park green
   - schools and **colleges** blue
   - shopping areas orange

2. If you lived in Bold St, list the streets you would pass on the way to Napia **Plaza**.

   _____

   _____

3. What would you find at the **corner** of Dean and Watt Streets?

   _____

   _____

4. What streets cross the railway line? _____

5. Name the streets that form a T **intersection** with Elizabeth St. _____

6. What town is to the north-west of Napia? _____

Spelling

Write six different words from this week's spelling list on page 72 then choose six interesting words in bold from this week's story that you'd like to learn to spell.

Class Spelling

Story Spelling

Spelling Activity: Circle the misspelt words.

activities   coleges   corner   intersecshion   dangarus   error   mobile   Zeeland

English – Proofreading

Correct the word usage and punctuation in these sentences. Write the corrections.

1. Why shouldnt them come?
2. He's name is rocky.
3. Dr marquez gave me an injection.
4. do happy children always laugh.
5. Cream puffs is very sweat.
6. He was Tammys pe teacher.
7. Mrs Garic has fore birds in a cayge.
8. I think Ill take today of school.

Unit 9 Homework Tonight 5

Maths – Knowledge/Skills

1. 32 + 22 = _____
2. Find the perimeter of a triangle with sides 6 m, 9 m and 14 m _____
3. Write 763 in expanded form: _____
4. 40 litres of petrol @ $0.75/L _____
5. What number comes 12 after 27 780? _____
6. Draw a triangular prism:
7. Give this shape a name: _____ 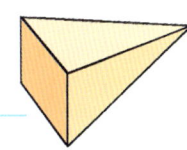
8. Arrange these numbers in rising order:
   13 690   13 906   13 096
   _____
9. _____ ÷ 7 = 4 r 5
10. 0.56 + 0.67 _____

Space and Geometry

Distance

Read the map; colour the sea blue, lowlands green and mountains brown.

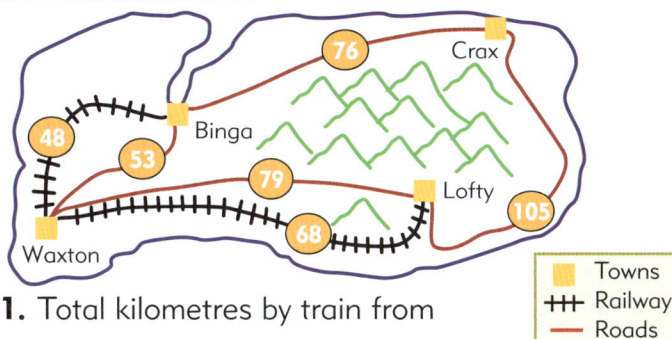

Towns: Crax, Binga, Lofty, Waxton
Distances: 76, 48, 53, 79, 68, 105

Legend: Towns, Railway, Roads

1. Total kilometres by train from Binga to Lofty: _____
2. Combined kilometres for car and train trip travelling from Crax to Waxton: _____
3. Distance from Binga to Lofty via Crax: _____
4. Total distance by road from Binga return around the island: _____

Number

1. 157,693
   94,708
   + 201,101

2. 54,702
   – 1,712

3. $57.63
   × 9

4. 6) 798

Research – New Zealand

Rearrange the Data Bank to form a summary describing New Zealand. _____

Label the map with place names from the data bank.

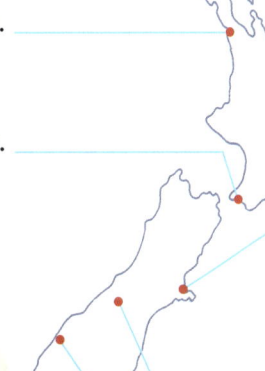

1. _____
2. _____
3. _____
4. _____
5. _____
6. _____
7. _____

Word Bank
- Stewart Island
- Mount Cook
- Milford Sound
- Rotorua
- Auckland
- Christchurch
- Wellington

Data Bank
- southern tip of the South Island. • New Zealand's two main islands, • lives on the North Island. • are separated by Cook Strait. • Two-thirds of New Zealand's population • Stewart Island is at the • North Island and South Island,

Child's Signature _____   Teacher's / Parent Signature _____

Unit **10** Homework Tonight 5   Text Type: Explanation

Reading – What's in a Watery Name?

Underline the correct word in each ( ) to help the story make sense.

Have you wondered just how some of the oceans and seas around the **1.** (map, place, world) got their names? **Usually** they tell us **2.** (sometimes, something, somewhere) about the nature of the sea in just the same way your name might say something about your **character**. Early **explorers** never saw **3.** (birds, bats, bandicoots) fly over the Dead Sea and thought the air above the sea was **poisonous**. Now we know that birds don't fly over **4.** (them, it, at) because it's a dead piece of water. Nothing lives in it. Not even fish, because it's **5.** (two, too, to) salty!

Heavy winter fogs which make the **6.** (water, sails, engines) look unusually gloomy and black gave the Black Sea in Europe its name. Fogs like this are **7.** (easy, hard, good) for us in this part of the world to **appreciate**. We usually enjoy a more **8.** (rainy, hot, pleasant) **climate**, so I wouldn't like to live close to the Black Sea, would you?

Can you guess why the sea near the **9.** (Grand, Great, Grey) Barrier Reef was named the Coral Sea? Of course you can; it's because large **10.** (coral, seaweed, drift wood) reefs are found in the area. Most seas around Australia however, are **11.** (found, nowhere, named) after explorers and remind us of brave and sometimes foolhardy **seafarers** from **12.** (yarns, yawns, years) gone by. All the seas on planet Earth have now been named, but if you found a **13.** (old, new, middle-aged) one, what name would you give to it? How would you **14.** (**decide**, deliver, deny)?

Q1: What is the main idea this passage is telling the reader? _____

_____

Q2: How would you decide on the name of a sea or ocean? _____

Spelling

Write six different words from this week's spelling list on page 72 then choose six interesting words in bold from this week's story that you'd like to learn to spell.

Class Spelling

Story Spelling

Spelling Activity: Cross out the wrong spelling in each pair.

posinus / poisonous   deside / decide   debt / dete   thieves / thiefs

English

An adverb can tell how, when, where or why. Using the word bank, write the most suitable adverb for each sentence.

1. The children ate _____
2. Natalie ate muffins _____
3. I live _____
4. She slept _____
5. Robin wrote _____
6. Therese hit the button _____

Data Bank
- yesterday • twice
- here • quickly
- carefully • deeply

26

Unit 10 Homework Tonight 5

Maths – Knowledge/Skills

1. Draw the lines of symmetry (fold lines) across this octagon.

2. Total days in April and May. _____

3. How many noughts do you have to add to make 4 into four thousand? _____

4. (3 × 8) + (4 × 11) = _____

5. $\frac{1}{4}$ of 48 = _____

6. $4^2 + 6^2$ = _____

7. An apple has a mass of 100 g or 1kg? _____

8. 27 ÷ _____ = 4 r 3

9. $1 - \frac{28}{100} = \frac{}{100}$

10. If Wednesday is the 26th May, write the date of the previous Thursday: _____

Space and Geometry

3D Shapes

1. Complete the isometric drawing, given the three views.

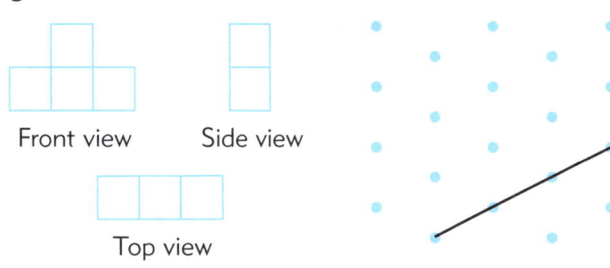

   Front view   Side view

   Top view

A number of blocks are placed on a table similar to the diagram.

How many faces could you see if there were:

2. 5 blocks _____   3. 8 blocks _____
4. 12 blocks _____   5. 15 blocks _____

Number

1. 18,930
   35,789
   + 57,289

2. 106.9
   – 59.0

3. 334
   × 11

4. 4) 257

Research – Seas & Oceans

Label these seas and oceans on a map of the world, colour the water blue.

Data Bank
- Pacific
- Indian
- Atlantic
- Antarctic
- Arctic
- Tasman Sea
- Timor Sea
- China Sea

The Big Question: What influences our tides? _____

Child's Signature _____   Teacher's / Parent Signature _____

Unit 11 Homework Tonight 5   Text Type: Factual Recount

Reading – My Brother's Car
Complete the story by using the code.

If you saw how my big brother 1. ✓✠✌✌✗✌ _____ over the four wheels parked in our driveway you would think it was a **Formula** 1 racing car. It's really a heap of junk which 2. ♦⚷▲➥▼✿ _____ goes and cost him all of $500. Mum and Dad said it wasn't a really good buy and he should have looked around and **investigated** prices a bit more. He didn't listen though and now it's parked, 3. ▼✗⚷■✚☐✤ _____ oil, right in front of my bedroom.

I like my big brother and I don't want to criticise him. He's trying to make the car look as **presentable** as 4. ❱✲✌✌✚✂▼✗ _____ and spends countless hours under the bonnet, fiddling with and **adjusting** everything that moves. Just as well his mate, Roberto, 5. ■☐✲✝✌ _____ something about **engines**.

Yesterday he told me that he needed to replace the **gaskets** in the **carburettor**. Roberto said it would be 6. ▲✗⚷▼▼✿ _____ easy and take only about two hours. Well, six hours later and with the driveway blocked, they still hadn't finished. It was getting dark and I had to hold an **emergency** trouble light so they could 7. ✓✚☐✚✌♦ _____ .

Dad **reckons** that with all the **practice** my big brother is getting 8. ▲✗❱⚷✚▲✚☐✤ _____ cars, he could open a garage. Don't know if I'd take my car to him – would you?

Q: Why do you think my brother bought the car in the first place? _____

Code	a	b	c	d	e	f	g	h	i	j	k	l	m	n	o	p	q	r	s	t	u	v	w	x	y	z
	⚷	✂	✐	➥	✗	✤	✚	♦	✠	●	■	▼	✿	☐	✲	❱	"	▲	✌	✄	✠	✝	✞	✟	☞

Spelling
Write six different words from this week's spelling list on page 72 then choose six interesting words in bold from this week's story that you'd like to learn to spell.

Class Spelling

Story Spelling

Spelling Activity: Supply the missing letters to these words and rewrite them correctly.

invest_gated   adju_ting   em_rgency   re_kons   c_ment

English
Add these position words.

1. Naomi crawled _____ the floor.
2. _____ the fire sat a weary hiker.
3. _____ the rock was a thriving colony of soldier ants.
4. The cat climbed up on the couch _____ Luke and me.

Word Bank
- beside
- underneath
- along
- between

Unit 11 Homework Tonight 5

Maths – Knowledge/Skills

1. 72 ÷ 9 = _____
2. Share 96 among 12 = _____

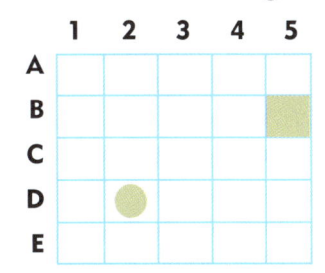

	1	2	3	4	5
A					
B					
C					
D					
E					

Write the grid reference for:

3. The circle = _____
4. The square = _____
5. How many halves in $7\frac{1}{2}$? _____
6. 7 'post it' pads cost $4.20. How much each? _____
7. Write 507 in expanded form: _____
8. (23 + 69) − (4 × 12) = _____
9. Write the multiples of 6 that are less than 45: _____
10. $3.65 × 100 = _____

Space and Geometry
2D Space

Complete this table of polygons:

Shape	Name	No. obtuse angles	No. of diagonals	No. of axes of symmetry
trapezium				
triangle				
hexagon				
pentagon				
parallelogram				

Number

1. 11,003
   92,050
   + 888

2. 875
   × 9

3. 6.977
   − 5.958

4. 3) 459

Research – Occupation

Match each occupation description with the name of the person following that occupation.

1. I repair motor vehicles. _____
2. I prescribe medicines. _____
3. I design roadways. _____
4. I help dancers with their dancing. _____
5. You will find me at a police station. _____
6. I drive government cars. _____
7. I love cooking. _____
8. I spend hours behind a camera. _____
9. I care for sick people. _____
10. I love displaying new clothes. _____
11. I'm good with a vacuum cleaner. _____
12. I write computer programs. _____

Person
• doctor • choreographer
• mechanic • chef • model
• detective • engineer • nurse
• chauffeur • photographer
• programmer • cleaner

Child's Signature _____   Teacher's / Parent Signature _____

Unit 12 Homework Tonight 5 Text Type: Information Report

Reading – Butterflies
Read the story, then mark the boxes 'True' or 'False'.

Butterflies taste things **through** their feet. They stomp up and down on a leaf **judging whether** this is a **suitable** place to lay eggs. Some butterflies lay their eggs together in a clump, while others try to be cunning and leave little **scattered** bunches of eggs. They hope this will keep them safer from **enemies** which might enjoy the eggs for dinner.

Butterflies have a long, hollow tube just like a drinking straw which they use to suck up food. This is called a proboscis and they can roll it up neatly when it's not in use.

Butterflies have their **'skeletons'** on the outside of their bodies. They don't have back bones, knee bones or toe bones as we do, but instead have a soft body on the inside, and a type of hard shell all over the outside.

1. All butterflies lay their eggs in scattered bunches.
2. Many creatures enjoy eating butterflies' eggs.
3. Butterflies can taste things with their proboscis.
4. Butterflies have backbones as we do.
5. The proboscis is like a drinking tube.
6. Butterflies suck up food with their proboscis.
7. Some butterflies lay their eggs in a clump.
8. Butterflies have an exterior hard shell.

Spelling
Write six different words from this week's spelling list on page 72 then choose six interesting words in bold from this week's story that you'd like to learn to spell.

Class Spelling

Story Spelling

Spelling Activity: Circle the misspelt word in each pair and copy out correctly.

through / thrugh   suitible / suitable   centre / center   nearly / nearlly

English
Choose one of the conjunctions to make the sentences read correctly.

1. He was a brilliant soccer player, _____ the referee sent him off for poor sportsmanship.
2. Patience _____ knowledge are needed to fix an old car.
3. Both boys worked long into the night, _____ they finally fixed the car.
4. You can watch TV _____ do your homework; the choice is yours!

Word Bank
- and • but
- yet • or

Unit 12 Homework Tonight 5

Maths – Knowledge/Skills

1. How many sides has a quadrilateral? _____
2. Number of years in five decades plus 5 years? _____
3. Water freezes at _____ °C
4. An egg's mass is 50 g or $\frac{1}{2}$ kg? _____
5. Complete a square pyramid sitting on top of a cube:
6. 154 days = how many weeks? _____
7. (6 × 6) + (58 − 3) = _____
8. Which is larger, $\frac{1}{2}$ or $\frac{2}{3}$? _____
9. Average of 21, 7 and 20. _____
10. How much for 100 stamps @ 50c each? _____

Measurement – Area

Select the best measurement of area from the data bank to match the following.

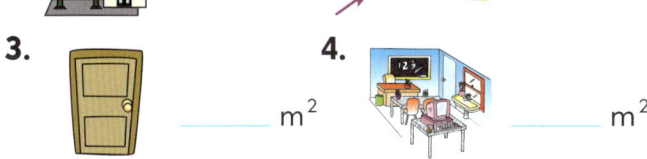

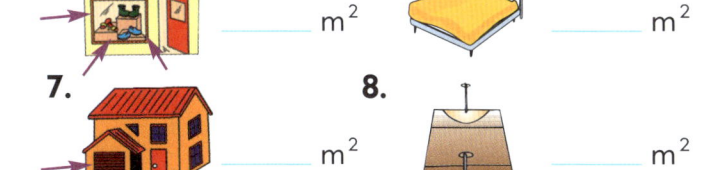

1. _____ m^2
2. _____ m^2
3. _____ m^2
4. _____ m^2
5. _____ m^2
6. _____ m^2
7. _____ m^2
8. _____ m^2

Data Bank • 260 • 6 • 600 • 60 • 10 • 44 • 2 • 4

Number

1. 4,345
   7,790
   5,629
   + 1,678

2. 7.090
   − 3.789

3. 12.67
   × 4

4. 9) 12.69

Research – Butterfly

Did you know?

- Over **1.** _____ species of butterflies exist worldwide.
- Butterflies fly during the **2.** _____ while most species of moth fly at night.
- Have **3.** _____ broad wings that close over the back at rest.
- A butterfly's wing is covered with thousands of **4.** _____ arranged in an **5.** _____ pattern like tiles on a roof.
- Colouring on a butterfly wing can: Help find **6.** _____ ; Serve as **7.** _____ ; Warn off predators.
- A butterfly is a beautiful adult for only **8.** _____ or days in a year long cycle.

Create and colour two different sets of butterfly wings.

Data Bank
• tiny scales • day
• camouflage
• overlapping • four
• 10,000 • a mate
• a few weeks

Child's Signature _____   Teacher's / Parent Signature _____

Unit 13 Homework Tonight 5   Text Type: Factual Description

Reading – Football Draw
Use the draw to answer the questions that follow.

Team	Home Ground
1. The **Warriors**	The Stadium
2. The Tigers	Central Park
3. The Reds	Red Stadium
4. The Broncos	Smith Park
5. The Bombers	The Oval
6. The Raiders	Raiders Stadium
7. The Knights	Powerhouse Stadium
8. The Bulldog Blues	Waratah Park
9. The Northerners	Gladiator Oval
10. **Conquerers**	Tower Oval
11. The Sharks	Sharks **Stadium**
12. The Lions	Lion Park

Round 1
1 plays 7
2 " 8
3 " 9
4 " 10
5 " 11
6 " 12

Round 2
12 plays 1
7 " 2
8 " 3
9 " 4
10 " 5
11 " 6

Round 3
1 plays 11
2 " 12
3 " 7
4 " 8
5 " 9
6 " 10

Round 4
10 plays 1
11 " 2
12 " 3
7 " 4
8 " 5
9 " 6

Round 5
1 plays 9
2 " 10
3 " 11
4 " 12
5 " 7
6 " 8

Round 6
8 plays 1
9 " 2
10 " 3
11 " 4
12 " 5
7 " 6

Round 7
1 plays 4
2 " 8
3 " 9
7 " 10
8 " 11
6 " 12

Round 8
6 plays 1
4 " 2
5 " 3
12 " 7
10 " 8
11 " 9

Round 9
1 plays 5
2 " 6
3 " 4
7 " 11
8 " 12
9 " 10

1. List the teams playing in these games:
   a) R1: 4 & 10 _____
   b) R3: 5 & 9 _____
   c) R5: 3 & 11 _____
   d) R9: 2 & 6 _____
2. Who will The Reds play in Round 4? _____
3. If The **Knights** played Western Sydney in Round 7 at home, where would they play?
   _____
4. Each team is **allowed** to fly 20 players to the game. If the adult fare from Sydney to **Melbourne** is $375 return, how much will the trip cost a Sydney team? _____
5. List the teams The Northerners team will play in the first 5 games: _____
6. In what round will The Bombers play The Warriors? _____

Spelling
Write six different words from this week's spelling list on page 72 then choose six interesting words in bold from this week's story that you'd like to learn to spell.

Class Spelling

Story Spelling

Spelling Activity: Supply the missing two letters to these words and write correctly.

co_q_er_rs   G_ad_ato_s   Wa_ri_rs   c_r_al   _gnor_nt   r_c_ive   _ou_h

English – Editing
Each line has two errors; list them in the grid provided.

1. Each player in the knew competition must attend train.
2. Only 20 players can be tooken to a match at any won time.
3. Im sure there are many others wating at home to take their places.
4. I wunder which teem will be the winner.
5. jack watched the game with grate interest.

Unit **13** Homework Tonight 5

Maths – Knowledge/Skills

1. 52 + 62 = _____
2. Write $3\frac{56}{100}$ as a decimal. _____
3. Divide the sum of 16 and 8 by 4. _____
4. Angles more than 90° are called _____
5. 4 books @ $8.80 each = _____
6. Draw the axes-of-symmetry fold lines on these two shapes:

7. 117 + 360 + 6 = _____
8. Radius of a circle is 5.5 cm. What is its diameter? _____
9. The area of a square is 81m². What is the length of each side? _____
10. Value of the 6 in 12.6: _____

Number – Subtraction

Fill in the missing numbers:

1. | H | T | U |
    |---|---|---|
    | 5 | 7 | ☐ |
    | –3 | ☐ | 2 |
    | ☐ | 2 | 6 |

2. | H | T | U |
    |---|---|---|
    | ☐ | 8 | 3 |
    | –2 | ☐ | ☐ |
    | 6 | 8 | 3 |

3. | H | T | U |
    |---|---|---|
    | 8 | ☐ | 6 |
    | –4 | 6 | ☐ |
    | ☐ | 2 | 6 |

4. Newlake to Pentagon = _____
5. Pentagon to Bethungra = _____
6. Bethungra to Oura = _____
7. Newlake to Oura = _____

F37
Newlake   56km
Pentagon   137km
Stumpy Head 205km
Bethungra 337km
Oura   596km

Number

1. 870
    1,042
    309
    + 7,642
    _____

2. 8,739
    – 2,588
    _____

3. 489
    × 8
    ____

4. 6) 1,014

Research – Games

Using the Data Bank, complete the descriptions of these games, then draw a suitable picture and name each one.

1. _____   2. _____   3. _____

Data Bank
- marble arches
- score
- kite flying
- Maori
- spinning tops
- Japanese

Draw a picture of the game.

Thread is twisted around a block shaped like a pear. Players whip the thread off and the block spins. Played by _____ children.

Draw a picture of the game.

Small round balls flicked through spaces in a box. Spaces are numbered and the highest _____ wins.

Draw a picture of the game.

Paper shapes tied to a string and flown in the breeze is a favourite game for _____ children.

4. Why do children invent new games? _____

5. What new game would you invent? Name it: _____

   Describe it: _____

Child's Signature _____   Teacher's / Parent Signature _____

Unit 14 Homework Tonight 5   Text Type: Factual Recount

Reading – Bail Up!   Tick one square in each set.

If you were **travelling** from any of the Australian goldfields in the 1850s to the 1880s, the sound you would fear most was: 'Bail Up!' Your coach would sway to a jolting stop and you would be **surrounded** by men with guns and deep voices telling you in no uncertain terms to get out of the coach and hand over your **valuables**.

One of the most valuable items carried by the coach would of course be its consignment of gold. Often this would be in a locked sea chest and carried on the back of the coach. A quick blast from one of the guns would remove the lock, and the canvas bags would be **snatched** away.

Where, might you ask, was the **armed guard**? Who would be so stupid as to send a single, horse-drawn coach along a bumpy dirt road with over a million dollars **worth** of gold?

Very often the police were simply **outnumbered**. Two or three guards against a dozen or so **desperate** men were no match. Sometimes a fallen log across the track stopped the coach and **escape** was impossible.

1. Hold-ups mainly occurred in
   a) the 1820s to the 1850s ☐
   b) the 1850s to the 1880s ☐
   c) the 1880s to the 1900s ☐

2. The coach carried
   a) a chest full of money ☐
   b) a chest full of guns ☐
   c) a consignment of gold ☐

3. The gold would be guarded
   a) by two or three men ☐
   b) by dozens of men ☐
   c) only by the driver ☐

4. The gold was carried
   a) on the back seat of the coach ☐
   b) on top of the coach in a chest ☐
   c) in canvas bags in a chest ☐

5. Circle two theme statements about the story: **horses are too slow / dangers of travelling in the 1800s in Australia / problems with transporting gold / trees along country roads**

Spelling
Write six different words from this week's spelling list on page 72 then choose six interesting words in bold from this week's story that you'd like to learn to spell.

Class Spelling

Story Spelling

Spelling Activity: Circle the misspelt words and rewrite them correctly.

valubles   consignment   snached   excape   kemist   explain   improove   trile

_____

English
Hyphens are used to break up words that are formed by joining two or more other words together. Rewrite these words and include the hyphen or hyphens.

1. pinup _____
2. twentyfour _____
3. brotherinlaw _____
4. proactive _____
5. wellliked _____
6. showoff _____
7. pre1994 _____
8. exteacher _____

Unit 14 Homework Tonight 5

Maths – Knowledge/Skills

1. (18 + 32) – (18 – 8) = _____
2. Write the next two numbers in the sequence: 315, 330, 345, 360, _____ , _____
3. Four centuries = _____ years
4. Write the time 3 hours before 5.30 on the clock face:
5. How many sides has a rhombus? _____
6. Which is the smaller, $\frac{1}{4}$ or $\frac{1}{3}$? _____
7. 150 BC to AD 1285 = _____ years
8. 4 + 62 = _____
9. 2^3 = _____
10. $(\frac{3}{4} - \frac{1}{2}) + (5 + \frac{3}{4})$ = _____

Measurement – Volume

Calculate the surface area of these boxes. They are not to scale.

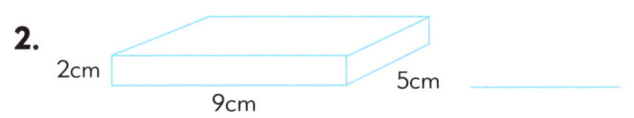

1. 2cm, 4cm, 5cm
2. 2cm, 9cm, 5cm

Abbreviations
Write the correct abbreviation for these measurements:

3. cubic centimetres _____
4. millilitres _____
5. square centimetres _____
6. kilometres _____

Data Bank • km • mL • cm^2 • cm^3

Number

1. 125
   345
   45
   + 107

2. 28.69
   – 24.98

3. 2,345
   × 9

4. 8) 6,727

Research – Convict Bushrangers

• Hobart • Sydney • Newcastle • Moreton Bay • Port Macquarie

Using the Phrase Bank, complete these sentences about convicts:

1. Escaped convicts were called bolters, _____
2. In 1832, Australia had 150 bushrangers _____
3. In the early days, police had no _____
4. Recaptured convict bushrangers were usually _____
5. Most convicts did not stay in gaol, but worked _____

Show five places where convicts were sent in Australia.
1. _____
2. _____
3. _____
4. _____
5. _____

Phase Bank
• bush robbers and later, bushrangers. • guns, horses or proper training. • on farms or roads and escape was easy. • flogged with the cat-o-nine tails. • and only 600 police to catch them.

Child's Signature _____   35   Teacher's / Parent Signature _____

Unit 15 Homework Tonight 5 — Text Type: Factual Recount

Reading – Ben Hall
Underline the sentence which does not belong in each paragraph.

Ben Hall was a **famous bushranger**. Many folk songs have been **written** about him because he was not **cruel** or violent. People have been fascinated by his **character** and wondered how he came to be a bushranger. Forbes is a town in New South Wales. Have you ever seen a **picture** of Ben Hall?

Not only did Ben Hall rob mail coaches but pastoral **stations** and even **whole** towns. In 1863 he took over the town of Canowindra in New South Wales for three days. Neville Hopper has dark brown hair. On separate occasions he stole twenty-three horses and took sixty men **prisoner**. We don't know what happened in these situations but it was **enough** for him to be declared an **outlaw** and shot on sight. Months later, that's exactly what happened. In a shoot-out with police he was killed – hit by thirty **bullets**.

1. Which town did Ben Hall take over? _____
2. For how long did he take it over? _____
3. How many horses did Ben Hall steal? _____
4. What did Ben Hall rob? _____
5. How did Ben Hall die? _____

Spelling
Write six different words from this week's spelling list on page 72 then choose six interesting words in bold from this week's story that you'd like to learn to spell.

Class Spelling

Story Spelling

Spelling Activity: Identify the misspelt words in this sentence by circling and rewrite the sentence correctly.

Hole towns were afraid of the crul and violent bushragers.

_____

English – Plural
Change these words into plurals. Be careful! Some just add 's' or 'es'; others are trickier!

box _____	lady _____	glass _____	sheep _____	shot _____
ox _____	potato _____	wolf _____	tooth _____	woman _____
man _____	hero _____	piano _____	cupful _____	
fly _____	reef _____	calf _____	child _____	

Unit 15 Homework Tonight 5

Maths – Knowledge/Skills

1. 23 + 57 + 64 = _____
2. $\sqrt{9}$ = _____
3. 30 − $\sqrt{25}$ = _____
4. $18.88 - $9.50 = _____
5. Find the mass of nine 49 g eggs. _____
6. 3 m 48 cm + 4 m 39 cm = _____
7. 89% = $\overline{100}$
8. 0.36 = _____ %
9. Write in words: $269.33 _____
_____
10. Shade 72% of this hundreds square.

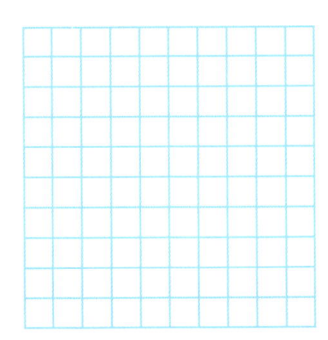

Data – Temperature

Graph these temperatures on the grid below:

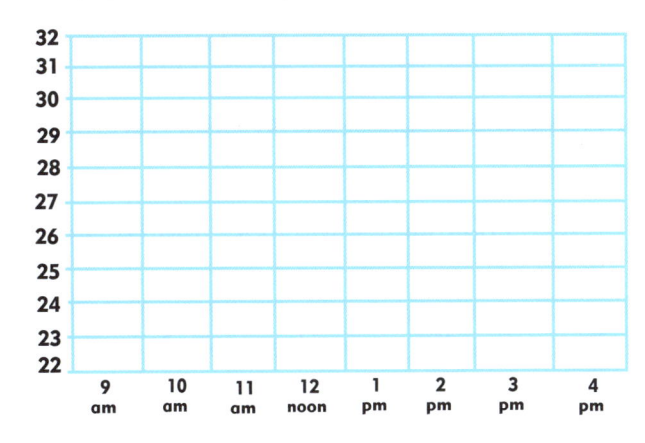

9.00am, 25°C   10.00am, 26°C   11.00am, 28°C
12.00noon, 28°C   1.00am, 30°C   2.00pm, 32°C
3.00pm, 30°C   4.00pm, 25°C

Number

1. 64,782
   29,048
 + 47,809

2. 235.8
 − 197.5

3. 2,505
  × 12

4. 5) 3,333

Research – Burns & firefighting

~~burns~~
chemical
superficial
deep
blister

inflammable
dressing
scald
extinguisher
hydrant

pyromaniac
smouldering
hazard
firefighter
appliance

Complete the word puzzle about burns and firefighting, then use some of the words to complete the sentences.

1. The fire was still _____ after a day.
2. Mum received a bad _____ from the steaming kettle.
3. We have a small fire _____ in the kitchen.
4. Fortunately, the boy only had _____ burns.
5. The hospital nurse applied a _____ and allowed him to go home.

B	A	S	G	H	S	T	B	C	Q	B	A
S	U	P	E	R	F	I	C	I	A	L	H
C	C	R	F	I	R	U	H	D	P	I	A
A	E	U	N	J	D	E	E	P	O	S	Z
L	X	W	E	S	Q	V	M	E	N	T	A
D	T	D	R	E	S	S	I	N	G	E	R
X	I	Y	D	K	P	W	C	F	M	R	D
I	N	F	L	A	M	M	A	B	L	E	Z
D	G	E	C	N	A	I	L	P	P	A	Y
G	U	P	Y	R	O	M	A	N	I	A	C
F	I	R	E	F	I	G	H	T	E	R	X
I	S	M	O	U	L	D	E	R	I	N	G
L	H	Y	D	R	A	N	T	G	L	R	W
M	E	Z	C	L	O	X	A	H	K	S	V
U	R	A	B	M	N	Y	Z	I	J	T	U

Child's Signature _____   Teacher's / Parent Signature _____

Unit **16** Homework Tonight 5   Text Type: Factual Description

Reading – Television Guide

NEW
4.00 Wondergirl (Final)
4.55 Kids' News
5.00 Captain **Midnight**
5.35 Cally's Kitchen
6.00 News

TAS
3.30 Everything Goes – Quiz
4.00 That's **Excitement** – Quiz
4.30 Cartoons
5.00 Schulz – R
5.30 Our Street – R
6.00 News

Pride
3.30 City life – R
4.00 **Dolphin** Tales – Nature
4.35 Beat the Buzzer – Quiz
5.00 Local Round-up
6.00 News and **Weather**

Global
3.30 Craft Corner
4.00 The Rats of Numph
4.30 **Wonderful** World – Nature
5.00 **Gamble** On – Quiz
5.30 Early News

1. Name the program **choices** you have when you came home from school at 4.00 p.m.
   _____

2. Which channel has the most quiz shows during the afternoon and what are they?
   _____

3. What does 'R' mean after a title? _____

4. Which channel has the **earliest** News **program** and what is it called? _____

5. Which program is the longest? _____

6. List the **nature** programs: _____

7. Which **channel** would you **prefer** to watch and why? _____
   _____

Spelling

Write six different words from this week's spelling list on page 72 then choose six interesting words in bold from this week's story that you'd like to learn to spell.

Class Spelling

Story Spelling

Spelling Activity: Write the missing letter in each word and rewrite on the line.

choi_es   nat_re   anc_ent   choc_late   famo_s   re_ular   tr_ly

English – Plurals

Each line has a spelling error and a punctuation mark or capital letter missing. Circle each mistake then write corrections.

Dear Unkle paul.
i really apreciated receiving your birthday
present today I didn't know you new that my
roller blads were broken. the ball-bearing
you sent fits just right. pretty unusual berthday
present, by I appreciate it very much
                    Thanks natalie

Unit 16 Homework Tonight 5

Maths – Knowledge/Skills

1. $50 - 7^2 =$ _____
2. Average 8, 38 and 20: _____
3. How many degrees between North and South? _____
4. Double 49 _____
5. How many degrees in a straight line? _____
6. 365 789 < 65 879 True or False? _____
7. How many hectares in 16 000m^2? _____
8. Colour Brown $\frac{2}{3}$ of this block of 24 squares of chocolate.
9. Kim had $2.50 for lunch but spent $\frac{1}{5}$ of it. How much did she have left? _____
10. How many minutes between 2.08 a.m. and 2.42 a.m.? _____

Number – Multiplication

Write the algorithm and answer for these problems:

1. A ferry carries 368 passengers on each of eight trips it makes each day. How many people altogether travel by ferry?

2. Computers in Wigham cost $2,769 each. If the Wigham College bought seven, how much would they spend?

3. Peta is a potter and supplies a box of pottery to eight stores each month. If each box contains five trays of 35 pieces, how many pieces would she need to make each month?

Number

1. 87,419
   9,307
   96,549
   + 3,821

2. $47.79
   − 22.99

3. $53.36
   × 11

4. 4) $7.36

Research – Television

Answer the questions and label the video camera.

1. Who was the father of television? _____
2. When did television come to your country? _____
3. When did we first see colour television in our country _____
4. _____
5. _____
6. _____
7. _____
8. _____
9. _____
10. What do you need to remember when making a good, clear video?

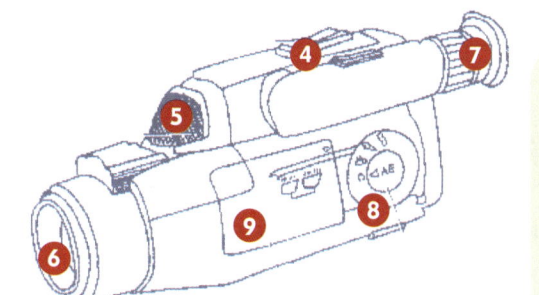

Data Bank for Labelling
- activating dial
- view finder
- power zoom
- video cassette
- microphone
- zoom lens

Child's Signature _____   Teacher's / Parent Signature _____

Unit 17 Homework Tonight 5
Text Type: Explanation

Reading – The Greenhouse Effect
Mark the statements T or F.

In the **atmosphere**, high above the Earth, light from the sun **streams** down towards the Earth. Before it reaches Earth, it passes through layers of gases. The sunlight warms the Earth and the sea, and this heat is **reflected** back up at the layers of gases. They trap this heat in the same way that a **greenhouse** traps warmth. This is why it is called the 'greenhouse' effect.

The greenhouse effect is normal and if we didn't have it, the **planet** would freeze and all the seas turn to ice. But at the moment, the planet is heating up too much. This is because the gases, **carbon dioxide**, methane and CFCs are building up in the atmosphere. These gases **absorb** too much heat from the sun. Where are these gases coming from? They are given off by car **exhausts**, the burning of coal, oil and gas, rotting **rubbish** and **aerosol** cans.

Are these statements about the greenhouse effect true or false?

1. Sunlight is reflected from the clouds.
2. There are layers of gas in the atmosphere.
3. The seas will turn to ice.
4. The greenhouse effect is not normal.
5. The gases trap heat from the Earth.
6. Carbon dioxide is building up in the atmosphere.
7. Rotting rubbish gives off gas.
8. We must stop the greenhouse effect completely.

Spelling
Write six different words from this week's spelling list on page 72 then choose six interesting words in bold from this week's story that you'd like to learn to spell.

Class Spelling

Story Spelling

Spelling Activity: Supply the missing letters to these words and write correctly.

str___ms   gr___nhouse   abs___b   exh___sts   ___oir   fa___ion   nucl___r   tu___el

English – Pronouns
Using the word bank, add the best pronoun to complete sentences. Write the sentence beginning with a capital letter if needed.

1. _____ is coming home after school?
2. _____ is the video we want to see.
3. "_____ book is this?" asked the teacher.
4. _____ will happen to her?
5. _____ plants are extremely rare.
6. To _____ are we speaking?

Word Bank • who • this • whom • these • whose • what

Unit 17 Homework Tonight 5

Maths – Knowledge/Skills

1. 23 + 57 + 88 = _____
2. Write seven-tenths as a decimal _____
3. $\frac{3}{4}$ of a year = _____ months.
4. $24.77 – $9.50 = _____
5. Write these numbers in ascending order
   78 346   87 456   86 345
   _____
6. Round 5 422 to the nearest hundred
   _____
7. What fraction of $50 is $25? _____
8. Find the average of 46, 49 and 4 _____
9. 6 years = _____ weeks.
10. Write the number these place-value clocks represent: _____

Measurement – Mass

If one cube has a mass of 3 units, find the mass of these blocks.

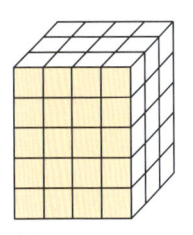

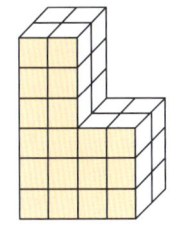

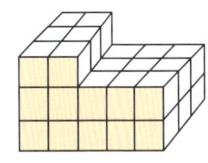

1. Mass
2. Mass
3. Mass
4. What is the difference between the lightest and the heaviest block? _____

Number

1. 7,892
   6,909
   + 9,241

2. 56.93
   – 16.79

3. $5.321
   × 5

4. 9)1111

Research – Pollution

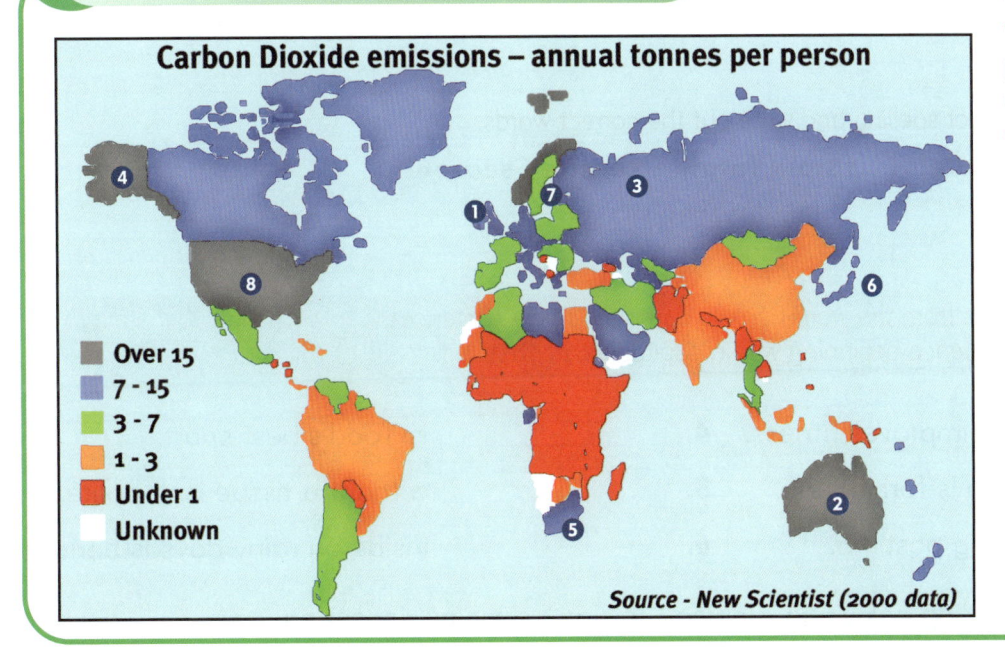

Carbon Dioxide emissions – annual tonnes per person

Over 15
7 - 15
3 - 7
1 - 3
Under 1
Unknown

Source - New Scientist (2000 data)

Locate these countries which were the worst carbon dioxide polluters in 2000. Match the numbers on the map to the countries.

☐ United States
☐ Russia
☐ Japan
☐ Alaska
☐ Australia
☐ South Africa
☐ United Kingdom
☐ Norway

Child's Signature _____   Teacher's / Parent Signature _____

Unit 18 Homework Tonight 5   Text Type: Procedure

Reading – Fire Safety

Read each paragraph and decide which sentence best expresses the main idea.

If you are asleep and the smoke alarm in your house **sounds**, don't rush blindly around in a **panic**. If you throw open your bedroom door and run into the **hallway** you may dash into smoke and flames. Take a **moment** to think and act cautiously. You may just save your life.

1. Get out of your bedroom quickly when the alarm sounds. ☐
2. Don't panic when you hear the smoke alarm. ☐
3. You may save your life if you're lucky. ☐

Touch the doorknob very **carefully** because it may be hot. If it is, this means that the fire is just outside the door. **Remain** in your room, open the window and call for help. Stuff **towels** or sheets in any gaps around your door to **prevent** smoke filtering into your room.

1. Don't burn yourself by touching a hot doorknob. ☐
2. You will be safer in your room if the doorknob is hot. ☐
3. Call for help when you hear the smoke alarm. ☐

Q. Why can breathing in (or inhaling) smoke be as dangerous as the actual fire?

Spelling

Write six different words from this week's spelling list on page 72 then choose six interesting words in bold from this week's story that you'd like to learn to spell.

Class Spelling

Story Spelling

Spelling Activity: Cross out the incorrect spelling and write out the correct words.

momant / moment   towls / towels   fatel / fatal   seeson / season

English

Choose words from the word bank to complete these sentences. Write the sentence beginning with a capital letter if needed.

1. _____ with a rope improves fitness.
2. _____ in this exam is forbidden.
3. _____ is an exciting pastime.
4. _____ is Todd's best sport.
5. _____ without a tissue isn't polite.
6. _____ inside on rainy days is boring.

Word Bank • sailing • playing • running • talking • skipping • sneezing

Unit 18 Homework Tonight 5

Maths – Knowledge/Skills

1. $7^2 + 6 =$ _____
2. $2\frac{3}{4} + 3\frac{1}{4} =$ _____
3. How many days in winter? _____
4. Find the area of this rectangle _____

   6 cm 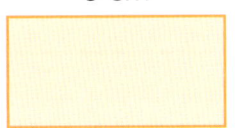 

   4 cm

5. Add $155 + $45. Change from $500 _____

6. Product of 6 and 5 _____
7. How many halves in seven? _____
8. ☐ x 15 = 45
9. How many 20c coins make $14.60? _____
10. 345 – 235 = _____

Measurement – Time

Draw the hands on the clock faces to show these 24-hour times as 12-hour times.

1. 13:53 
2. 17:37 
3. 22:14 
4. 15:38

5. What is the time 15 minutes before midday? _____

6. What is the time 30 minutes before 9.30 a.m.? _____

Number

1. 1,347
   23,589
   + 3,672

2. 44.44
   – 5.55

3. $912
   x 7

4. 12) 666

Research – The setting sun

Data Bank – Diagram
- scattered blue light
- scattered red light
- atmosphere
- person
- sun overhead
- sun low in the sky
- the Earth

Label this diagram to show the effect of the atmosphere on the light rays from the sun as they pass through the atmosphere.

1. _____
2. _____
4. _____
3. _____
6. _____
7. _____
5. _____

Data Bank – Story
- light
- sky
- scattered
- shines
- orange
- thickness

Earlier and later in the day, the sun 8. _____ through a greater 9. _____ of atmosphere than when it is overhead. At these times, the 10. _____ turns an 11. _____ – red colour because the photons of red and orange 12. _____, which are of a lower energy level than the blue photons, are 13. _____ low in the atmosphere.

Child's Signature _____   43   Teacher's / Parent Signature _____

Unit 19 Homework Tonight 5   Text Type: Procedure

Reading – Cooking

These ingredients are correct, but the steps to make the rice bubble caterpillars are in the wrong order.

Write the method in the correct order, then complete activities.

Ingredients:
box of Rice Bubbles
4 spoonfuls of butter
1 packet of marshmallows
currants, licorice pieces, peppermints
pipe cleaners
aluminium foil
electric fry pan, 1 spoon

Method:
- Put butter on fingers to mould the shape
- Tear off a 30 cm square of **aluminium** foil
- Melt butter in the frypan
- Stir in rice bubbles to make a stiff **mixture**
- Scoop out mixture to shape into a **segmented** caterpillar
- When melted, stir in marshmallows
- Add sweets for eyes, etc.
- Continue **stirring** until they are melted
- Turn off frypan
- Add pipe cleaner lengths for legs

Steps in correct order:
1. M _____
2. W _____
3. C _____
4. S _____
5. T _____
6. T _____
7. S _____
8. P _____
9. A _____
10. A _____
11. What safety rules would you have to remember? _____

12. Describe the most difficult part of this work and what you would do to solve the problem.

Spelling

Write six different words from this week's spelling list on page 72 then choose six interesting words in bold from this week's story that you'd like to learn to spell.

Class Spelling

Story Spelling

Spelling Activity: Supply the missing letters to these words and write them out correctly on the line provided.

m _ thod   alumi _ ium   mi _ ture   ele _ tric   citi _ en   interv _ l   obedi _ nt   t _ re

English

In each of these sentences, there is an incorrect word and a misspelt word. Make the corrections. Use the data bank. Just write the correct words.

1. My laser computer produces crisp, cleer copies. _____
2. Memories of myself encounter with Big Foot are vivide. _____
3. Good cooking requiring car and patience. _____
4. Russell's lawnmover makes an almighty rocket!

Word Bank
- my • clear
- printer • vivid
- lawnmower • care
- requires • racket

Unit 19 Homework Tonight 5

Maths – Knowledge/Skills

1. Write one-and-a-half million in figures _____

2. What shape is an orange? _____
3. Beverley turned 20 in 2002.
   In what year was she born? _____
4. Find the area of a rectangle 11 cm long and 8 cm wide _____
5. Cross out the incorrect word.
   An angle of 110° is acute / obtuse.
6. 82 × 22 = _____
7. How many years in three-quarters of a century? _____
8. What is the name of the fold-line down the centre of a shape when the two sides fold on top of each other? _____
9. Lou had $5.00 to spend. He spent $\frac{1}{10}$ of it; how much did he spend? _____
10. Average these daily temperatures:
    31°C, 24°C, 28°C, 33°C, 28°C,
    27°C, 25°C, _____ °C

Working Mathematically – Number Crossword

Across:
1. Weeks in a year
2. Days in 1995
5. $\frac{1}{2}$ of 550
6. 7^2 =
8. Three score =
9. A baker's dozen
11. 144 + 6 =
12. Half of seven thousand, **then** minus 500

Down:
1. 5 × 11 =
3. Six thousand five hundred and twenty-nine
4. Days in September
7. 9^2 + 25 =
10. 6^2 − 3 =
11. Years in a decade

Research – Cooking

Items: 1 mixing bowl, grater, sharp knife, frypan, wooden spoon
Ingredients: 500g mince, 1 carrot, 1 egg, cooking oil

Use these items and ingredients to produce your own meat balls!

Step 1 _____
Step 2 _____
Step 3 _____
Step 4 _____
Step 5 _____
Step 6 _____
Make a list of the types of food you would eat with meatballs _____

Draw a picture of your finished meal. Add a table setting to complete the picture.

Child's Signature _____ Teacher's / Parent Signature _____

Unit 20 Homework Tonight 5
Text Type: Discussion

Reading – "Get off the Phone!"
Choose the best of the three words to complete the story.

I'm sure that if you're a **normal** young person who just 1. (hates / loves / looks) to keep in contact with your friends, you have heard this comment over and over again. Sometimes it 2. (really / ready / unreal) **infuriates** you, but other times you know you've been on the 3. (fax / computer / phone) too long, and finish your **conversation** and hang up.

My question is: "What do you do with people who give you a 4. (easy / hard / wrong) time over this?" I guess it depends on two things. Who it 5. (is / are / isn't) asking you to hang up and the importance of your conversation. Right! OK, it's your Dad and he's been **patient** for about half an 6. (year / second / hour) waiting to use the phone and he asks you to get off the phone. What do you do? My guess is that because you're a 7. (horrible / small / reasonable) person, you simply say, "OK, Dad!", tell your friend you'll get back to them later and hang up.

However, what say it's your **irritating** younger brother or sister? I 8. (guess / give / guest) you might ask, why they want to use the phone anyway? I bet you say, "In a minute!", and one minute draws out to two minutes and then three minutes until 9. (he'll / they're / they) at it again – "Get off the phone!"

I hope you don't blow your stack, but 10. (never / simply / **sample**) count to ten and remember that others have rights too – no matter how young they are! Perhaps it's one of the prices you 11. (pay / provide / put), having to use the family phone when you want to talk to your friends. **Imagine** what life would be like with your own 12. (motor / **mobile** / radar) phone.

Q: What problem is outlined here? _____

Spelling
Write six different words from this week's spelling list on page 72 then choose six interesting words in bold from this week's story that you'd like to learn to spell.

Class Spelling		Story Spelling	

Spelling Activity: Circle the spelling errors in this sentence and write the words correctly.

I stood under an umbreller to resku the dry clowthing from the washing line.

_____

English
Select the males that go with these females.

1. princess _____
2. mistress _____
3. squaw _____
4. cow _____
5. sultana _____
6. sorceress _____
7. heifer _____
8. nun _____
9. mare _____
10. heroine _____
11. giantess _____
12. heiress _____

Word Bank
• prince • brave
• hero • monk
• steer • giant
• master • heir
• stallion • bull
• sorcerer
• sultan

Unit **20** Homework Tonight 5

Maths – Knowledge/Skills

1. $45.00 ÷ 9 = _____
2. What number is halfway between 3000 and 4000? _____
3. Find the average of $9, $15, $4 and $8 _____
4. Draw a shape with 3 acute angles

5. Two score and 3. How many? _____
6. $\frac{4}{10}$ of 2 metres = _____ cm
7. How many hectares in a square kilometre? _____
8. 4 kg 530 g + 3 kg 470 g = _____ kg
9. Write one thousand, four hundred and eight in figures _____
10. The perimeter of a rectangle is 58 metres. If one side is 19 metres, how long is the other side? _____

Number – Fractions

Colour the part of each group indicated by the fraction.

1. $\frac{5}{9}$ 2. $\frac{3}{5}$ 3. $\frac{3}{10}$

4. What would be the result of adding $\frac{3}{5}$ of one bucket to $\frac{4}{5}$ of another bucket, the same size? _____

5. If I add $\frac{3}{4}$ of one box of corn flakes to $\frac{5}{8}$ of another box of the same size, how much would I end up with? _____

Number

1. 23,480
   89,002
   + 90,990

2. 3,098
   − 674

3. 90,704
   × 6

4. $\frac{3}{4}$ × 8 = ___

Research – Telecommunications

Complete these statements by unjumbling the word in brackets. First letters are given.

1. Telephones send and receive sound by means of e_____ (itlryecciet).
2. The word telephone comes from two Greek words t_____ (eelt) meaning far and p_____ (oepnh) meaning 'sound'.
3. Many telephone messages today travel by m_____ (acrwvmoei).
4. Printed messages can be sent by telephone, using a f_____ (icmlasife) machine.
5. S_____ (tselisalet) are used to send telephone messages over long distances.
6. M_____ (eiolmb) phones are useful by people on the move.
7. Telephone handsets contain both permanent and electro (temporary) m_____ (ngesmta).

The Big Question: How has the Internet changed our use of the telephone?

Child's Signature _____   47   Teacher's / Parent Signature _____

Unit 21 Homework Tonight 5   Text Type: Explanation

Reading – My Pony

Choose from the word bank a similar word to the one in brackets, to complete the story.

I bet some of you have a **1.** (small) _____ **model** horse at home called 'My Pony'. Bronwyn and Natalie have. It has a long tail and mane which needs **combing** **2.** (every) _____ day. I've seen some of you comb 'My Pony' for hours and hours. Your older brother must get really turned off by your **3.** (regular) _____ combing of the pony.

Still, you like your pony and no-one, not even your **4.** (older) _____ brother can tell you to play with something else. If he does, **5.** (advise) _____ him to mind his own business. Your pony probably has lots of **brilliant** colours and that makes him really special, but let me **6.** (picture) _____ my pony.

My pony lives in my mind. No, he's not a ghost pony, and not even something that appears at times and disappears at other times. He is really the sum total of all the horses I have ever seen and lives **7.** (**entirely**) _____ in my mind.

I sit and dream of my pony. I close my eyes and let him **gallop**. Together we can **8.** (leap) _____ over low scrub and gallop along the beach.

After our **9.** (quick) _____ run along the beach we canter home where I unsaddle my pony and break open a new bale of **lucerne** hay. I brush down his flanks and talk **10.** (carefully) _____ to him as I make him **comfortable** and give him my total **concentration**.

As I dream on and read more and more of my **favourite** horse **11.** (newspaper) _____, I can actually feel the gentle warmth of my horse's **12.** (body) _____ and smell the freshly cut hay. It all seems so very real… but that's the power of my **imagination**!

Q: How can I keep from annoying my brother? _____

Word Bank • flank • gently • completely • describe • big • each • magazine • brisk • jump • tell • miniature • constant

Spelling

Write six different words from this week's spelling list on page 72 then choose six interesting words in bold from this week's story that you'd like to learn to spell.

Class Spelling			Story Spelling	

Spelling Activity: Circle the misspelt words and write them correctly.

brilliant   gallep   concentration   imaganation   flava   sandwich   unaform   horse

_____

English

Match these colloquialisms with their meanings.

1. At a loose end _____
2. Hard up _____
3. Good for nothing _____
4. Under a cloud _____
5. The man in the street _____

Data Bank
• nothing to do
• an ordinary person
• in trouble
• useless
• short of money

Unit 21 Homework Tonight 5

Maths – Knowledge/Skills

1. $27 ÷ 2 = _____
2. Write the time $2\frac{1}{2}$ hours after 8.30 a.m. _____
3. How many right angles in a rectangle? _____
4. A prism has these sides; length 5 cm, width 4 cm and height 3 cm. What is the volume? _____
5. List the prime numbers between 10 and 22 _____
6. What is the number half way between 4000 and 5000? _____
7. This object is built of centimetre cubes. How many cm³ altogether? _____ 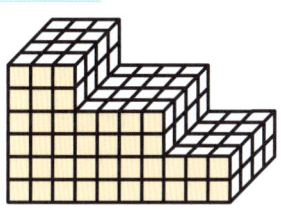
8. Find the perimeter of an isosceles triangle with a 7cm base and sides measuring 11cm _____
9. (34 x 3) + (21 x 2) = _____

Number – Fractions

Complete this table of cost price, sale price and profit.

	Cost Price	Selling Price	Profit
1. 	$36.65	$45.80	$ _____
2. 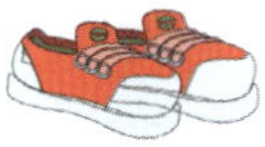	$48.50	$62.00	$ _____
3. 	$2050	$2525	$ _____

Calculate 10% discount on these items:

4. $45.00 $ _____
5. $37.50 $ _____
6. $19.25 $ _____

Number

1. 19,346
   10,030
   + 7,986

2. 1030
   − 928

3. 825
   x 9

4. 6) 1446

Research – Horses

Match statements from the data bank with the most appropriate horse. Draw and label one of the horses.

Data Bank
• help round up cattle • quiet nature
• can turn quickly • bred and trained to race
• able to pull loads • can cost a lot of money

Draw one of these horses.

Carriage Horse
_____
_____
_____

Race Horse
_____
_____
_____

Stock Horse
_____
_____

Type of horse: _____

Child's Signature _____   Teacher's / Parent Signature _____

Unit 22 Homework Tonight 5   Text Type: Factual Description

Reading – Dictionary
Study this **dictionary** page carefully and complete the activities.

HEED		
heed	(v. t.)	attend to; take **notice** of (n); care, attention
heel 1	(n)	hinder part of **human** foot; part of a sock that covers; well supplied with money
heel 2	(v)	(of a ship) lean to one side; make heel
hegemonic	(a)	supreme
heifer	(n)	a young cow that has not had a calf
height	(n)	**measure** from base to top; elevation above the ground or sea **level**; high **point**; top; utmost degree
heighten	(v. t.)	raise higher; intensify; exaggerate
heir	(n)	person entitled to property or rank as legal representative of former holder
helical	(a)	spiral
helicopter	(n)	flying **machine** with horizontal rotating blades.
heliograph	(n)	signalling apparatus reflecting **sunlight**
heliotrope	(n)	plant with small clustered purple flowers; **colour** or **scent** of these
helium	(n)	a gas, first inferred in sun's atmosphere.
helm	(n)	tiller or **wheel** for managing **rudder**; the steerage; guidance
helmet	(n)	defensive head-cover; upper part of retort

1. What is a heifer? _____
2. One word for 'a signalling apparatus reflecting sunlight'. _____
3. Give two meanings for 'heel'. _____
4. What can you add to the meaning of 'helicopter' to tell something about the direction of its flight? _____
5. In what kind of order are these words? _____
6. Why is the word 'HEED' in capital letters at the head of the page?
_____

Spelling
Write six different words from this week's spelling list on page 72 then choose six interesting words in bold from this week's story that you'd like to learn to spell.

Class Spelling

Story Spelling

Spelling Activity: Provide the missing letters to complete the words.

meas _ _ _   mach _ _ _   esc _ _ _   dict _ _ _ ary   forbid _ _ _   ordin _ _ _

English
Choose one of the nouns from the word bank to make the sentences read correctly.

1. A small, dainty _____
2. My plastic _____
3. Three huge _____
4. A wild stormy, _____
5. A boiling pot of _____
6. A ringing _____

Find words in the word bank to make rhyming pairs:

7. screen _____
8. trip _____
9. fool _____
10. house _____
11. laser _____
12. puzzle _____
13. night _____
14. reading _____

Word Bank • mouse • night • stew • waves • seeding • flower • muzzle • mean • model • razor • telephone • tool • hip • light

Unit 22 Homework Tonight 5

Maths – Knowledge/Skills

1. How many halves in $3\frac{1}{2}$? _____
2. What is used to measure temperature? _____
3. Colour $\frac{7}{8}$ of this square.
4. 135 − (sum of 23 and 37) = _____
5. If two lines run side by side, but never meet they are _____
6. $21.78 + $34.35 = _____
7. Halve 86 _____
8. Weeks in 5 years _____
9. Share $7.02 amongst 9 people.
10. Use a numeral to replace the two boxes.
    ☐ × ☐ = 9

Data – Graphing

Complete this graph showing these race times in the City to Surf. Times are in minutes. Luigi 93, Ben 98, Jacki 103, Jade 87, Katie 67.

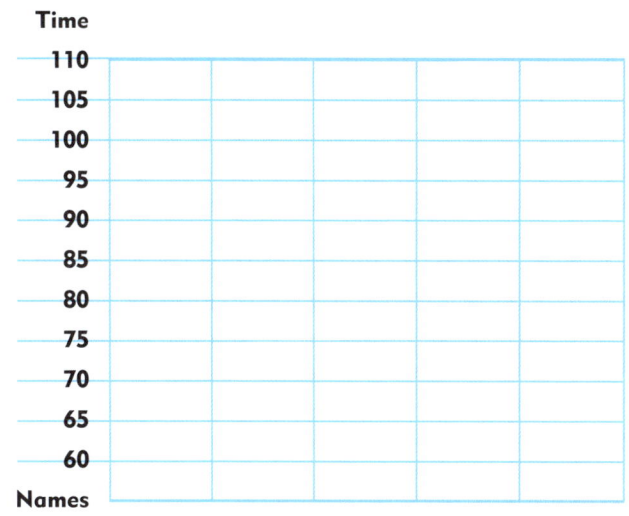

Time
110
105
100
95
90
85
80
75
70
65
60
Names

Number

1. 93.39
    98.42
    103.48
    87.25
    + 67.35

2. 103.48
    − 67.35

3. 94.1
    × 12

4. 5) 449.85

Research – Tasmania

Complete information about Tasmania.

General

Tasmania is one 1. _____ the size of 2. _____ and the same size as 3. _____.
It is fairly 4. _____ but with some lowland 5. _____.

6. _____
7. _____
8. _____
9. _____
10. _____

Farming/Land Use Locations

11. sheep grazing _____
12. wilderness areas _____
13. dairy and cheese _____
14. fruit and cattle _____

Data Bank – General
• plains • Ireland
• Victoria • third
• mountainous

Data Bank – Locations
• Hobart • Launceston
• Devonport • Bass Strait
• Queenstown

Data Bank – Farming
• midland areas
• northern areas
• southern areas
• west coast areas

Unit 23 Homework Tonight 5

Text Type: Observation

Reading – Bugbear

Decide whether the statements about the story are true or false.

In the world of computers the name Bugbear puts fear, **terror** and frustration into the hearts of all computer owners. Bugbear isn't a huge **insect** or even a small bear — it's a computer **virus**.

Bugbear isn't a very destructive virus. It's more annoying than anything else because it attaches itself to addresses in your address book and keeps sending off to other people parts of **e-mails** you have both sent and received. After coming into contact with Bugbear your computer needs a really thorough clean out.

How can a computer catch a virus? Does it **float** through the air or does it come from another computer? Mostly viruses come as e-mail attachments via the Internet. Checking files and e-mails for viruses should be done on a **regular** basis. An up-to-date virus checker should be used and viruses destroyed immediately.

	True	False
1. Bugbear is a destructive virus.	☐	☐
2. The virus is floating in the air.	☐	☐
3. Bugbear destroys bears.	☐	☐
4. The virus can spread from one computer to another.	☐	☐
5. Bugbear ruins the hard drive.	☐	☐
6. A virus checker kills the virus.	☐	☐

Spelling

Write six different words from this week's spelling list on page 72 then choose six interesting words in bold from this week's story that you'd like to learn to spell.

Class Spelling

Story Spelling

Spelling Activity: Circle the misspelt words and rewrite correctly.

teror   virus   e-males   float   reguler   arange   oxygen   usualy

English – Analogies

Choose words from the data bank to complete these analogies.

1. Spider is to fly as cat is to _____
2. Tear is to sorrow as smile is to _____
3. Wrist is to arm as ankle is to _____
4. Artist is to _____ as author is to book.
5. Sheep is to mutton as pig is to _____
6. Moon is to Earth as Earth is to _____
7. Tired is to sleep as dirty is to _____
8. Computer is to printer as phone is to _____

Word Bank • painting • leg • Sun • wash • Internet • mouse • happiness • pork

Unit 23 Homework Tonight 5

Maths – Knowledge/Skills

1. 888 ÷ 2 = _____
2. (5 x 103) + (3 x 102) = _____
3. $\frac{3}{4}$ of 48 = _____
4. $\sqrt{81}$ = _____
5. Draw an object which is 1 cm x 1 cm x 2 cm.

6. Write two million in numerals _____
7. How many days in spring? _____
8. Average of 14, 26, 15 and 25 _____
9. How many axes of symmetry has a square? _____
10. 5 x 20 x 5 = _____

Space and Geometry

3D Space

Complete this table:

Object	Edges	Corners	Curved surfaces	Does it spin?
1. (cone)				
2. (cube)				
3. (cylinder)				
4. (sphere)				

Draw the net of a cone and a square pyramid in this space.

Number

1. 234,560
   5,090
   + 67,120
   _____

2. 123.56
   – 56.97
   _____

3. 34.9
   x 8
   _____

4. $\frac{3}{4}$ x 60 = __

Research – Computer

Using the data base about computers, write a statement to match each picture.

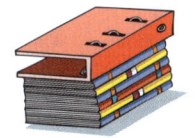

1. _____
2. _____
3. _____

4. _____
5. _____
6. _____

Data Base
• computers help cars run smoothly • computers help big planes fly
• shop without carrying money • computers help organise information
• computers make learning fun • chat with friends on the Internet

Child's Signature _____   Teacher's / Parent Signature _____

Unit 24 Homework Tonight 5 Text Type: Personal Response

Reading – Fact or Opinion
Write "F" if these are facts, "O" if they are opinions.

1. **Bananas** have more flavour than apples.
2. Kakadu National Park is in the **Northern Territory**.
3. **Perth** is the **capital** city of Western Australia.
4. A comet killed all the **dinosaurs** on Earth.
5. Ants have six legs.
6. **Chocolate** is really delicious.
7. Fruit and **vegetables** help to keep you **healthy**.
8. No-one ever gets 100% in a spelling test.
9. The Moon moves in an orbit around the Earth.
10. Cricket is the best sport to play in summer.
11. Tyrannosaurus rex was a meat-eating dinosaur.
12. Cricket matches are televised during the summer months.
13. London is in **England** and Paris is in **France**.
14. A lot of television **programs** are not worth watching.
15. Television programs include soapies, quizzes and news.

Spelling
Write six different words from this week's spelling list on page 72 then choose six interesting words in bold from this week's story that you'd like to learn to spell.

Class Spelling

Story Spelling

Spelling Activity: Which word in the pair is incorrect? Write out the correct word.

bananas / bananus   chocalate / chocolate   programes / programs   vallies / valleys

English
Name the contents of these containers, using the Word Bank.

1. purse _____
2. basin _____
3. sheath _____
4. cask _____
5. decanter _____
6. cup _____
7. briefcase _____
8. safe _____
9. vase _____
10. wardrobe _____
11. sack _____
12. tank _____

Word Bank   • sword • flowers • money • wine • tea • drink • petrol
• clothes • water • potatoes • papers • valuables

Unit 24 Homework Tonight 5

Maths – Knowledge/Skills

1. $15.00 + $13.50 + $6.75 = _____
2. $\sqrt{49} + 1 = $ _____
3. $\frac{7}{8} + \frac{1}{8} = $ _____
4. 5 kilograms and 670 grams = _____ g
5. Colour $\frac{5}{8}$ of this circle. 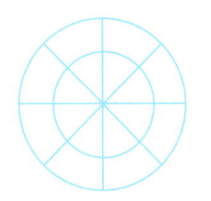
6. $61.60 ÷ 7 = _____
7. Round 246 891 to the nearest thousand: _____
8. Write the numeral for a quarter of a million _____
9. Is 15 a prime number? _____
10. Find the perimeter of a square with sides $4\frac{1}{2}$ cm _____

Number – Division

Complete these algorithms. All have remainders.

1. 3) 9,457
2. 6) 8,552
3. 4) 5,090
4. 7) 6,906
5. 8) 5,061
6. 4) 1,111

Find the missing numbers:

7. 3) ☐ ☐ ☐ → 2 1 6
8. 6) ☐ ☐ ☐ → 1 2 4 r 4

Number

1. 23,457
   3,509
   98,021
   + 6,111

2. 27,560
   − 7,666

3. 159
   × 7

4. 309
   × 6

Research – Dinosaur Remains

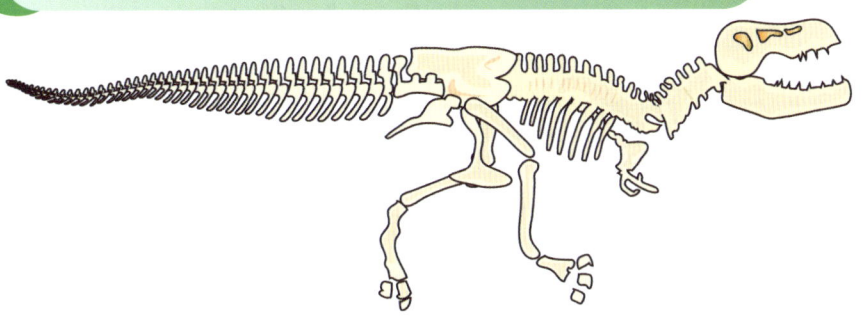

Complete the passage with words from the Data Bank, to tell you how scientists treat dinosaur remains.

Data Base
• exposed • jigsaw • uncover • air
• quarrying • reveal • skeleton • rock
• value • cleaned • tools • clinging

Dinosaur remains are often **1.** _____ because of a cliff fall when **2.** _____ or road works are being undertaken. Sometimes mining activities **3.** _____ fossils. Before more damage occurs, palaeontologists gather to carefully **4.** _____ the bony remains. It is a slow and painstaking task, because a whole **5.** _____ may be buried deep inside the **6.** _____ face. If the find is to be of **7.** _____ , every fragment must be collected, **8.** _____ and labelled. Chemicals are sometimes used and small **9.** _____ that vibrate and chip away the **10.** _____ rock are used along with blasts of **11.** _____ to wipe away the dirt. Then the **12.** _____ of the dinosaur's skeleton can be constructed.

Child's Signature _____   55   Teacher's / Parent Signature _____

Unit 25 Homework Tonight 5   Text Type: Procedural Recount

Reading – Bike Business
Underline the sentence which does not belong in each paragraph.

To ride your **bicycle** safely, you must have a good **knowledge** of the road rules. When riding in the streets of your town or city, **obey** the Stop and Give Way signs. Clean your car regularly. Don't **engage** in any reckless or silly **behaviour** when you are riding along the roadway or you may have (or cause) an accident.

Your bicycle must be in good mechanical **condition** with brakes which function efficiently. A working bell to warn **pedestrians** of your approach is necessary. If you **intend** to ride at night, a light and a **reflector** or tail-light will ensure that cars can see you. Some people like to surfing and others prefer walking.

1. Do bike riders have to obey the same rules as cars do, e.g. Stop signs? _____
2. Why shouldn't you ride a bicycle without brakes? _____
3. What do you need to ride safely at night? _____
4. Why is 'showing off' on your bike very foolish? _____
5. Which type of bike do you prefer to ride and why? _____

Spelling
Write six different words from this week's spelling list on page 72 then choose six interesting words in bold from this week's story that you'd like to learn to spell.

Class Spelling		Story Spelling	

Spelling Activity: Each word is misspelt. Write them correctly.

nowlege   condishion   bycicle   obay   forteen

English
Add 'self' or 'selves' to the word in bold to complete the sentence.

1. He made **him** _____ very busy.
2. My budgerigars are preening **them** _____ .
3. It went by **it** _____ .
4. Will you be able to help **your** _____ ?
5. Tye and I went by **our** _____ .
6. The cliff **it** _____ was enormous.
7. I fixed the computer all by **my** _____ .
8. She **her** _____ was talking.
9. The musicians **them** _____ came to the children's ward.

Unit 25 Homework Tonight 5

Maths – Knowledge/Skills

1. Write $\frac{23}{50}$ as a percentage: _____
2. 500 g of a sausage at $6.80/kg: _____
3. 6 score and 19 equals _____
4. 30 litres of petrol at $0.65/L: _____
5. Write 9835 in words: _____
6. How many degrees in 2 right angles?
7. Write the shaded part of this shape as a fraction: _____ 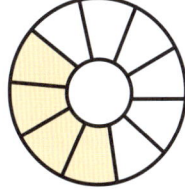
8. 12679 < 12769. True or False? _____
9. Yin was born in 1983. How old was he in the year 2000? _____
10. 7 x 50 x 2 = _____

Data – Co-ordinates

Look at this map of Treasure Island and colour the sea blue.

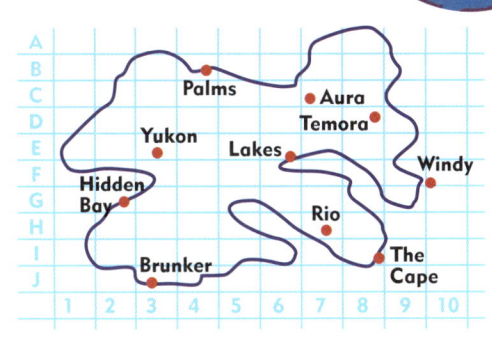

Towns on map: Palms, Aura, Yukon, Temora, Lakes, Windy, Hidden Bay, Rio, Brunker, The Cape

Write the town or location identified by these co-ordinates:

1. B4 _____
2. F10 _____
3. J3 _____
4. C7 _____
5. H7 _____
6. E3 _____
7. I8 _____
8. E6 _____
9. D8 _____
10. G2 _____

Number

1. 94,935
   98,047
   85
   + 5,031

2. 923
   − 496

3. 1,040
   − 444

4. $\frac{5}{8} \times 64 =$

Research – Aboriginal Rock Art

Copy the Koori art in this box.

List some implements Koori artists might use to complete an art piece.

1. _____

What subjects would Koori artists draw or create?

2. _____

What other forms of native art are found in the S-E Asian/Pacific region?

3. _____

Child's Signature _____   57   Teacher's / Parent Signature _____

Unit 26 Homework Tonight 5   Text Type: Factual Description

Reading – A Telephone Bill

	Your **Account** Number Z87 76 3289 6778 3 634	Date of Issue 09/03/2004	
Total of Last Bill $167.45	We received $167.45	**Balance** $0.00	Total of this bill $129.35
	Mr G. M. I. Rich 236 Eucalyptus Drive, Water Bay NSW 2680		**Payment** due by 27/03/2004

Account Summary
Service and **Equipment**
Calls and Charges
  Flexi-Plan Details
  02 Select Saver
	to 8th Mar
	Discount
		8th Feb to 8th Mar	$
			14.15
			0.00
			2.27CR

		Total Flexi-plan Balance	2.27CR
Services Summary Telephone Service Z87 76 3289 Metered Calls STD **Information** Calls	8th Feb to 8th Mar 119 units @ $0.25 each see details below see details below		 29.75 53.83 12.87
		Total for Z87 76 3289	$96.45
Telecard 2897635 NEVILLE HOPPER			
National Direct **Dialled**		see details below Total for 2897635	15.45 $15.45

Itemised Call Details   STD Calls

Date	Time	Place	Number	Rate	Min:Sec	$
Telephone Service Z87763289						
10 Feb	06:36pm	Sydney	028345456	Night	2:19	0.65
11 Feb	05:10pm	Sydney	028768654	Day	0:44	0.36
12 Feb	07:45pm	Wagga	069765435	Night	0:23	0.21
13 Feb	10:29pm	Clinton	079433454	Economy	23:08	4.19
15 Feb	11:15am	Sydney	023355666	Day	2:27	0.94
19 Feb	09:35am	**Brisbane**	073234949	Day	1:26	0.65
25 Feb	07:46am	**Adelaide**	083324555	Night	8:26	2.93

1. What service costs $15.45 for the month? _____
2. How much was the Select Saver discount? _____
3. Give details of the one economy call. _____

Spelling

Write six different words from this week's spelling list on page 72 then choose six interesting words in bold from this week's story that you'd like to learn to spell.

Class Spelling

Story Spelling

Spelling Activity: Add the missing letters to these words. Write them out correctly.

Br_sb_n_   A_ela_d_   e_ui_me_t   p_y_en_   d_sc_s_ed   s_rv_c_

English

Circle the three adjectives in the box, then write each in a sentence.

1. _____
2. _____
3. _____

- cupboard • shy
- ran • phone
- worried • answers
- fearful • raincoat

Unit 26 Homework Tonight 5

Maths – Knowledge/Skills

1. A millennium is _____ years.
2. Draw a rectangular prism
3. Round 4 m 35 cm to the nearest metre _____
4. 0.2 of a tonne = _____ kg
5. 5 × (5 + 3) = _____
6. A pentagon has _____ points.
7. Cross out the incorrect word
   An angle of 55° is acute/obtuse
8. 0.67 of $1 = _____ c
9. What fraction of a century is one year? _____
10. Write 18 903 in words _____

Working Mathematically – Value for Money

Consider the following problems. Show your algorithms and provide the answer.

1. If meat is sold at $8.80 per kilogram, but available in bulk at $55.00 for 10 kg, what is the total saving when buying 10 kg?

2. Mars Bars are $1.20 each. However, a bag of 20 costs $18.50. What is the saving when buying 20? _____

Number

1. 29,138
   14,914
   24,153
   + 11,811

2. 1,401
   − 712

3. $21.89
   × 11

4. 10) 9,476

Research – Categories

Separate the data into the correct category.

ANIMAL	VEGETABLE	MINERAL

Word Bank
- cougar • sloth
- quartz • artichoke
- calcite • yam
- lemur • aniseed
- gypsum • diamond
- graphite • marrow
- bok choy
- mongoose • lynx

INSECT	BIRD	FISH

Word Bank
- bee • rosella
- kiwi • trout
- cod • ant
- eagle • bream
- mosquito

Child's Signature _____   Teacher's / Parent Signature _____

Unit 27 Homework Tonight 5 — Text Type: Narrative Explanation

Reading – Four Eyes
Select the best phrase for each space to complete the story.

Belinda has four eyes. Two hazel and two blue. Two made of crystalline and two made of **plastic**. Two that can 1. _____ along with a wicked grin and two that just sit there and stare at you. Whoever heard of someone looking like this? I know you're pulling my leg. But wait, no, Belinda is a real-live person and a friend of mine. And, yes, she does have four eyes – she wears glasses. Not any sort of glasses, mind you, but 2. _____ _____ that she uses for reading.

Maybe you have heard of Belinda's glasses and maybe you know someone who also wears special glasses to 'keep the print still'. You see, Belinda 3. _____. Glare and bright, shiny-white pages are Belinda's worst enemies and **unfortunately**, the two come together when she opens most books and finds black print on white pages.

Something from the page is 4. _____ , telling her to look away from the page, it's hurting her eyes. She gets sore eyes, the print seems to **wander** all over the place and she often loses her place. At the same time her brain, and usually her teacher, is saying "**Belinda**, don't be silly, of course you can't stop. You have to read the page. Try harder and GET ON WITH IT!"

Of course the battle continues, the **statement**: "This hurts my eyes and 5. _____ , I may as well give up", is up against: "Of course you need to read this **information**. Try harder." Well, the battle is now under control with Belinda's new specs. Her world is taking on a whole new feel. "The print stays still with my new glasses," says Belinda, "I don't lose my place and I can read… simply 6. _____ and fourth eyes!"

Q: What was Belinda's real problem? _____

Data Bank • because of my very special third • special blue-coloured glasses • has a problem with too much light • wink at you • I'm losing my place • screaming out

Spelling
Write six different words from this week's spelling list on page 72 then choose six interesting words in bold from this week's story that you'd like to learn to spell.

Class Spelling

Story Spelling

Spelling Activity: Circle and rewrite the misspelt words.

plastik   wander   satment   infomation   domestik   shield   vilent

English
Indicate whether the verb (underlined) is past, present, or future tense.

1. Stephanie drew a picture. _____
2. Humans will land on Mars. _____
3. Men landed on the Moon. _____
4. Cars drive along expressways. _____
5. Seven singers will arrive. _____
6. My computer is playing up. _____

60

Unit 27 Homework Tonight 5

Maths – Knowledge/Skills

1. Write the difference between 23°C and 9°C _____
2. 6 × ☐² = 600
3. Five score minus 9 = _____
4. If you add all the angles of a triangle, the total will be _____ °
5. Write these times on the analog clock

   0840 hrs   0309 hrs
6. What is 10% of $15.00? _____
7. $3\frac{1}{5} + 5\frac{3}{5} =$ _____
8. How many axes of symmetry in a hexagon? _____
9. Fill in the next number: 3, 7, 15, 31, _____
10. Arrange these numbers in rising order
    22 020, 20 200, 22 220, 20 202

Measurement – Mass

Complete the table, showing mass written in various forms.

	Grams	Kilograms and Grams	Decimal Notation
1.	1600		
2.		4kg 150g	
3.	5920		
4.			2.8kg
5.			6.125kg

Change these to numerals:

6. seventy grams _____
7. two hundred and thirty grams _____
8. one thousand, four hundred grams _____
9. three kilograms and six hundred and seventy grams _____

Number

1. 246,890
   20,609
   + 507,614

2. 506.79
   − 37.89

3. 26
   × 12

4. 5) 40,501

Research – The Eye

1. m _____
2. c _____
3. f _____
4. r _____
5. l _____
6. i _____
7. b _____
8. o _____
9. s _____
10. What is an ophthalmologist? _____
11. Describe the work of the Fred Hollows Foundation: _____

Label the eye parts. Use an encyclopedia or the Internet to help you. Colour each section.

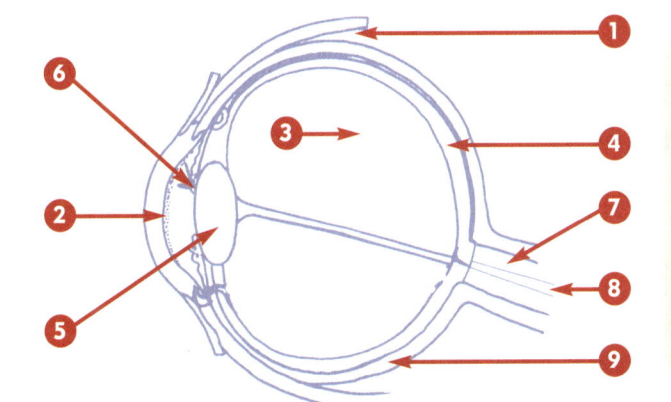

Word Bank
- cornea
- retina
- muscle
- iris
- optic nerve
- lens
- fluid
- blood supply
- sclera

Child's Signature _____   Teacher's / Parent Signature _____

Unit 28 Homework Tonight 5 Text Type: Factual Description

Reading – Mosquito World
Read this information about Mosquito World, the directions on how to find the place, opening times and entry costs.

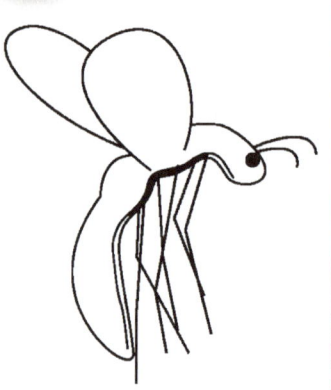

Mosquito World offers a full day of fun and **entertainment** for all ages, only 1½ hours (approx.) drive from the GPO – bring the whole family for a biting good time!
Coming from Riverview: Drive along Muddy Road, past the Swampy Golf Club. 1.3 **kilometres** on the right-hand side is the Mosquito World sign, turn left into the **property**.
Coming from Hometown: **Proceed** along the F106 Freeway, take Clay Road exit. Mosquito World is 5.8 kilometres along on the right-hand side.
Coming from the Mountain: Drive down Maria Drive to the Great Eastern Road. Turn left and go 3 kilometres, then turn right into Little Bite Road. Follow it to the end of Muddy Road. Turn right and **approximately** 4 kilometres on your left is Mosquito World.

OPEN 7 DAYS FROM 9.30 a.m. to 7.30 p.m. AND ALL PUBLIC HOLIDAYS
Monday and Tuesday for Educational **Purposes**
The Mosquito Band performs daily at 2.30 p.m.
Admission Prices: **Adults**: $13.50   Children: $7.50 (3-12 years)
                Pensioners: $10.00   Family: $35.00 (2 adults & 2 children)

Answer the questions.

1. If my average driving speed is 56 km/h, how far is Mosquito World from the city centre?

2. What roads are mentioned in the directions? _____

3. How far is the Swampy Golf Club from Mosquito World? _____
4. What happens at Mosquito World on Mondays and Tuesdays? _____

5. What happens at Mosquito World at 2.30 p.m.? _____
6. How much would it cost a group of 5 adults, 2 pensioners and 6 children to visit? _____
7. Would Mosquito World be open on Boxing Day? _____

Spelling
Write six different words from this week's spelling list on page 72 then choose six interesting words in bold from this week's story that you'd like to learn to spell.

Class Spelling

Story Spelling

Spelling Activity: All these words are incorrectly spelt. Write them correctly.

mosketo   proparty   admishion   adultes   kilomatres

English
Rewrite this text with the correct punctuation.

are we all going to visit newcastle for the match of the day between the newcastle knights and the auckland warriors asked kent excitedly you bet replied maui well give them a game to remember

Unit 28 Homework Tonight 5

Maths – Knowledge/Skills

1. What is the special name for 100? _____

2. Value of the 3 in 4 305 291? _____

3. List prime numbers between 18 and 30 _____

4. How many tenths in 5.7? _____

5. Double 38 _____

6. $6^2 - 16 =$ _____

7. How many days in spring? _____

8. One lunar year = _____ months

9. Draw a net for a square prism

10. (6 x 5) – (12 x 2) = _____

Geometry – Space

1. Draw a mirror image of this shape:

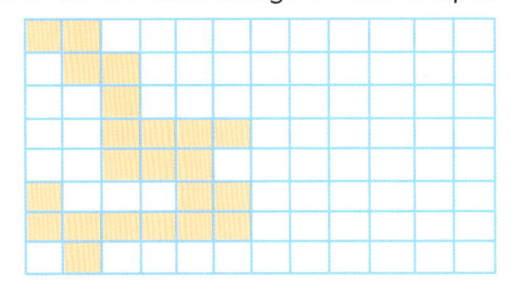

2. Draw this image rotated 90°:

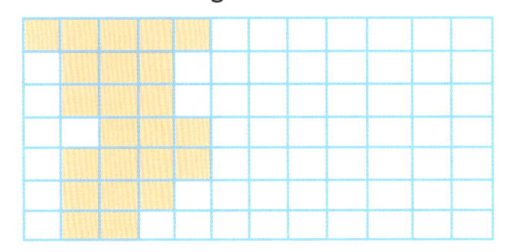

Number

1. $376.41
   $207.89
   + $769.22

2. 3,076
   – 2,107

3. 162
   x 2

4. $\frac{1}{2} + \frac{3}{4} =$ _____

Research – Mosquito

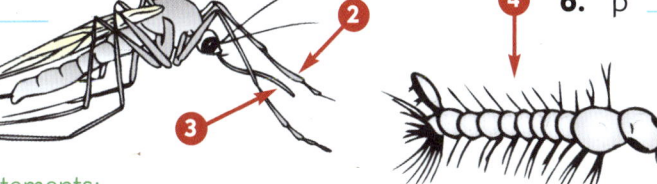

Label these diagrams.

1. a _____
2. b _____
3. s _____

4. l _____
5. b _____
6. p _____

Write true or false to these statements:

1. The mosquito is a flying insect. _____
2. Male mosquitos suck blood. _____
3. Mosquito saliva stops blood clotting. _____
4. Female mosquitos lay eggs below the surface of water. _____
5. All mosquitos carry dangerous diseases. _____

Question: How long for a larva to become a mosquito?
_____

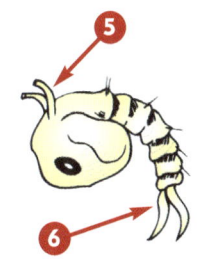

Data Base
• pupa • breathing tube
• larva • sucking tube
• balancing legs
• antenna

Child's Signature _____   Teacher's / Parent Signature _____

Unit **29** Homework Tonight 5   Text Type: Factual Description

Reading – Happy Holidays
Study the postcard and answer the questions.

> 24/10/04
>
> Dear Tory,
> Our flight was great! We flew across New Zealand and then on to Fiji. Now we are in our hotel – it's **glorious**. Sally and I have our own **separate** room next to Mum and Dad. There are two pools and the beach is a short walk away. We're going to an **extinct volcano** tomorrow. I love Fiji. Shopping at the markets is **terrific**!
>
> Your friend,
> Alison
>
> Tory Kendall
> 241 Ryan Street
> Lewisville NSW 2306
> AUSTRALIA

1. Is Tory on holidays? _____
2. What is Sally's sister's name? _____
3. Where is Alison on **holidays**? _____
4. How did she travel there? _____
5. What other country did the children fly across? _____
6. How many people are in Alison's family? _____
7. What will the family do tomorrow? _____
8. Do you think Alison likes shopping? _____
9. List 2 of four places Alison is sure to visit? _____
10. In what part of Australia does Tory live? _____

Spelling
Write six different words from this week's spelling list on page 72 then choose six interesting words in bold from this week's story that you'd like to learn to spell.

Class Spelling

Story Spelling

Spelling Activity: Circle the incorrect words. Write them out.

balance   concirn   glorius   glitter   position   xtinct   holerday   wealth

___

English
Write the most suitable predicate for each of these subjects, using the data bank.

1. Dark clouds _____
2. Sharon _____
3. Miserable adults _____
4. Hermit crabs _____

Data Bank
- make life hard for children
- threaded the needle carefully
- gathered overhead
- are seldom seen

Unit 29 Homework Tonight 5

Maths – Knowledge/Skills

1. How many degrees between south and south-east? _____
2. 65 ÷ 5 = _____
3. Write 34 690 in words _____
4. Express 6 kg 467 g as a decimal _____
5. Complete: A straight line is the shortest distance between _____
6. $\frac{56}{100}$ = _____ %
7. Write 9, 12 and 23 as ordinal numbers _____
8. What instrument is used to measure angles? _____
9. Draw an oval:

10. Draw the hands for 1450 hrs on this analog clock.

Measurement – Area

Measure these shapes to the nearest centimetre, then fill in the spaces and find the area.

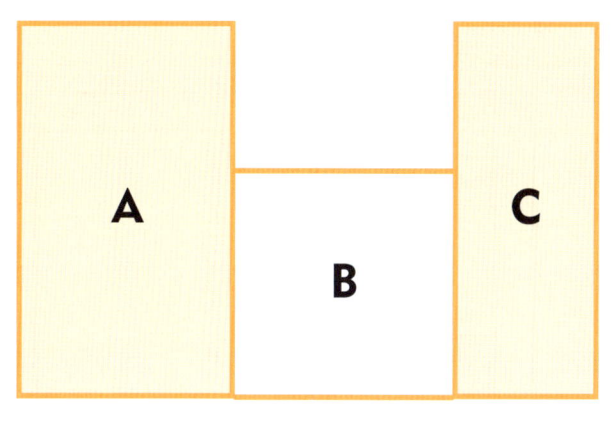

A   B   C

Area A = (_____ x _____) = _____
Area B = (_____ x _____) = _____
Area C = (_____ x _____) = _____
                    Total = _____

Number

1. 11.76
   142.31
   + 92.84
   _____

2. $50.00
   – $19.89
   _____

3. $47.20
      x 8
   _____

4. 9) 3,006

Research

Put these events and dates on the time line frame below.

1901 Federation of Australian States
1840 Treaty of Waitangi
1642 Abel Tasman sighted New Zealand
1880 Ned Kelly, the bushranger, hanged
1815 Road over the Blue Mountains built
1882 Dunedin transported frozen meat to England
1860 First Taranaki War
1854 Eureka Stockade battle

1   2   3   4   5   6   7   8

Shade Australian events green and New Zealand events blue.

Child's Signature _____   Teacher's / Parent Signature _____

Unit 30 Homework Tonight 5   Text Type: Factual Description

Reading – Credit Cards

Look at this credit card account, then complete the activities.

The Bank PO Box zzz, in your Capital City

Credit Card

For **enquiries** call: (002) 341 9047
Opening Balance: $1267.34

Date	Description	Location	Amount $
160204	Rob Stacker Auto SR	Hometown	20.00
170204	**Electric Appliances**	Novel East	450.00
220204	**Adjustment** of Credit Charges		0.50 -
230204	Boatclub **Foundation**	Hometown	125.60
250204	Twins Point Beach	Charlesville	25.50
250204	Payment **Received** Thank You		550.00 -
270204	The Vase Flowers	East Miles	18.65
280204	Hometown Motors	Hometown	75.90
020304	NRMASS	Kathay	35.00
100304	Ellersleys Sales	Charlesville	230.00
100304	**Lambs** Timber	Hometown	79.00
110304	Tyres Plus	East Miles	349.00
	Bank Fees		15.37
120304	Credit Charges		9.68

1. List the towns in which credit was issued. _____
2. What is the opening balance of the credit account? _____
3. List the purchases made on the 10th March, 2004. _____
4. What is the amount for adjustment of credit charges? _____
5. To whom are the credit charges paid? _____
6. What is the closing balance of the credit account? _____

Spelling

Write six different words from this week's spelling list on page 72 then choose six interesting words in bold from this week's story that you'd like to learn to spell.

Class Spelling

Story Spelling

Spelling Activity: Supply the missing letters to these words and write correctly.

el_ctri_   fo_ndati_n   rec__ved   fin_nci_l   ba__oon   gl_r_ous

English

Match these adjectives with these nouns.

1. accurate   m _____
2. careful   d _____
3. disposable   n _____
4. loyal   g _____
5. friendly   g _____
6. happy   c _____

Data Base
- nappy • guards
- children • guides
- driver • measure

Unit 30 Homework Tonight 5

Maths – Knowledge/Skills

1. Shade $\frac{1}{2}$ of this circle:

2. $\frac{1}{2}$ = _____ %
3. 1 millenium = _____ years
4. How much for 7 jars of peanut butter @ $2.80 a jar? _____
5. What 3D shape is this book? _____
6. Value of the 6 in 4.96 _____
7. 45 cm = _____ mm
8. $\frac{1}{2}$ thousand x 2 = _____
9. How many 500 mL containers fill $2\frac{1}{2}$ L? _____
10. Find the perimeter of a window width 2.4 m and height 1.3 m _____

Data – Graphs

Colour the squares to show on the graph car sales from this second-hand car yard for one week.

Key: $ = $1000 worth of cars sold

Ford	$8000
Toyota	$10000
Holden	$5000
Nissan	$7000
4WD	$9000
Trucks	$6000
Subaru	$5000

Number

1. 30,001
    41,008
     9,110
    + 9,090
    _____

2. $124.90
   – $99.65
   _____

3. $124.00
    x 12
   _____

4. 7) 7,090

Research – Money

From Stones to Coins.

Before the use of coins and notes, the following were used for trading:

1. _____ , _____ , _____ .

Last century in Australia, 2. _____ was turned into coins.

Many traders and storekeepers used their own

3. _____ tokens which were not
4. _____ but the government allowed their use.

In 1865, the Adelaide Assay (or gold office) produced gold
5. _____ . Each one was stamped by the
6. _____ with the correct
7. _____ .

Copy or make a rubbing of 2 modern coins.

Word Bank
- weight
- shells
- ingots
- legal tender
- government
- stones
- gold
- salt
- penny

Child's Signature _____ Teacher's / Parent Signature _____

Unit 31 Homework Tonight 5   Text Type: Factual Recount

Reading – Tangled Tails
Number these sentences from 1 to 8 to show the proper sequence of events.

1. a) The bike went faster and faster.
   b) **Luckily**, Amanda fell on grass and only winded herself.
   c) The bike hit the kerb.
   d) Amanda went for a ride on her **bicycle** and **ignored** Dad's **advice**.
   e) The brakes failed half-way down.
   f) She decided to coast down a long hill.
   g) Dad warned Amanda that the brakes were **defective**.
   h) Amanda flew over the handle bars.

2. a) He played with it at lunch-time.
   b) No-one knew what had happened to it.
   c) Jack borrowed his brother's GAME-BOY without asking **permission**.
   d) What would he do now?
   e) While playing handball, he put the GAME-BOY down.
   f) He took it to school to show his friends.
   g) Jack forgot all about it when the bell rang and he went to class.
   h) After school Jack searched frantically for it.

Spelling
Write six different words from this week's spelling list on page 72 then choose six interesting words in bold from this week's story that you'd like to learn to spell.

Class Spelling

Story Spelling

Spelling Activity: Write the six **bold** words from the story in alphabetical order.

English
Put the most suitable verb into each space in these passages.

1. Boris _____ a wet sponge at the teacher _____ in front of the target.
2. I _____ Sasha some extra work to _____ before tomorrow.
3. Phillipa _____ the softball as Erik _____ to the base.
4. Don't _____ so gentle with the ball as it's made to be _____ hard.

Word Bank • complete • threw • sitting • raced • gave • dropped • be • kicked

Unit 31 Homework Tonight 5

Maths – Knowledge/Skills

1. How many hectares in 35 000m²? _____
2. What 3D object is a Mars Bar? _____
3. 502 – (product of 4 and 6) _____
4. What 3D object is a coconut? _____
5. A straight line has 150°. True or False?
6. Write 6.35 a.m. in twenty-four hour time _____
7. Label the points on the compass
   N, S, E, W, NW, NE, SE, SW 
8. $4.66 × 7 = _____
9. 0.71 – 0.45 = _____
10. Express $5\frac{2}{100}$ as a decimal _____

Number – Fractions - Decimals

Complete this fraction table.

	Hundreds	Number over 100	Tenths & Hundreds	Decimal	Percentage
1.	77		T H		
2.		$\frac{65}{100}$	T H		
3.			T H	0.27	
4.			4T 3H		
5.			T H		83%

Colour

6. $\frac{2}{5}$ 7. $\frac{2}{3}$

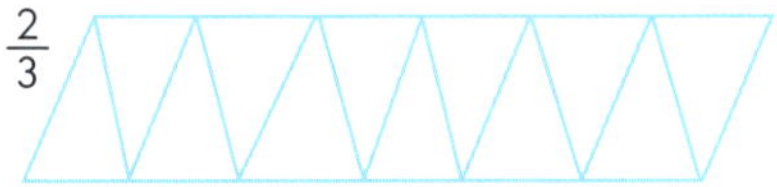

Number

1. 89,476
   94,874
   89,748
   + 68,894

2. 1,946
   – 957

3. 147
   × 7

4. 6) 1,839

Research – Lightning

Lightning Facts

1. Fast-moving raindrops in a cloud _____ _____ and create electricity.
2. Clouds, which build up lots of _____ send sparks to the ground producing _____ and _____ called lightning.
3. Distance to a thunderstorm can be measured by multiplying _____ metres for every _____ seconds _____ the lightning and the thunder.

Trace over this pattern of lightning flashes to the ground.

Draw Thor, the god of thunder, racing across the sky.

Word Bank
• electricity • rub together • between • light • two • heat • 800

Unit 32 Homework Tonight 5 Text Type: Information Report

Reading – The Great North Walk

A 250 km walking track from Sydney to **Newcastle** is one of the lasting **monuments** of the Bicentennial Year of 1988. It was designed for people of all ages and levels of **experience**. You can select day trips, weekend trips or complete the 14-day **venture** in one hit!

Some of the most **scenic** countryside in NSW can be found along the Great North Walk, with the route skirting Sydney Harbour, Lake Macquarie and the Newcastle coastline. Around the Hawkesbury River area, the track takes in a path to Berowra Waters and a boat trip to Patonga Wharf. Entering the Brisbane Water National Park provides access to some of the most **impressive** state forests in NSW.

Bush campsites are provided along the route, but you usually need to take care of your own toilet needs – behind a tree which is at least 150 metres from a watercourse! The track passes by shops where you may **purchase** additional supplies. If you are tired of camping, you may even find a motel. In more remote areas however, your five-star accommodation will be in a simple tent beside a quiet stream.

In order to begin the Great North Walk you need a spirit of discovery, the **necessary** willpower and the appropriate maps. Remember, take out only **photographs** (and memories) and leave behind only footprints.

1. List six of the areas the Great North walk passes through. _____

2. How do you get from Berowra Waters to Patonga Wharf? _____
3. What facility is not provided along the track, and why would this be the case? _____

4. What would you expect to see in an 'impressive' state forest? _____
5. Why is it important to remember to leave 'only footprints'? _____

Spelling

Write six different words from this week's spelling list on page 72 then choose six interesting words in bold from this week's story that you'd like to learn to spell.

Class Spelling

Story Spelling

Spelling Activity: Add the missing letters to these words and write correctly below.

New __ __ tle   exp __ ien __ __   vent __ e   i_pres __ ve   p __ ch __ __   n _ c _ s _ ary

_____

English

Find the two incorrectly spelt words in each sentence, and rewrite them correctly.

1. My mums a trifik mum. _____
2. Melanie hates strawbery jam on her bred. _____
3. We all want to Pete's for a piza last night. _____

Unit 32 Homework Tonight 5

Maths – Knowledge/Skills

1. Rewrite this fraction leaving out the non-significant zero: 08.01 _____
2. How many months in $1\frac{3}{4}$ years? _____
3. A plane is flying at 360 km/h. How far will it travel in 30 minutes? _____
4. What is a reflex angle? _____
5. Draw a square pyramid
6. The diameter of a circle is 3.8 cm. What is the radius? _____
7. List the prime numbers between 15 and 30 _____
8. Write $\frac{6}{8}$ in its lowest terms _____
9. Was 1989 a leap year? _____
10. If bricks cost $680 per thousand, how much for 5000? _____

Working Mathematically – Calculator

Use a calculator to answer these questions:

1. Square 14 and add 11 _____
2. Subtract 186 from the product of 21 and 28 _____
3. Divide 4094 by 46 _____
4. Square 3.8 _____
5. Multiply 7.9 by 15 _____
6. From the sum of 295 and 135, subtract 319 _____

Fraction Order

Write these decimal fractions in ascending order

7. 3.3   3.17   3.25   3.01   3.68
8. 0.163   0.258   0.188   0.217   0.199

Number

1. 1,594
   101,936
   19,824
   + 376,810
2. $140.00
   − $98.37
3. $73.29
   × 7
4. 11) 1,213

Research

Across
2. Another name for a path
4. A large body of water
5. You should carry _____ rations
7. On a hike you sleep in a _____

Down
1. You can carry food in a _____
3. Take _____ of the natural resources in the bush
4. Everything you carry should be _____
6. Know how to read a _____

Complete this outdoor adventure puzzle.

Word Bank
- labelled • light
- map • care
- lake • road
- emergency
- tent • pack
- enough • track

Child's Signature _____   Teacher's / Parent Signature _____

Year 5 Spelling Homework Tonight 5

List 1
aboard
battery
continue
eighth
guard
lightning
prisoner
skipping

List 2
absence
beginner
conversation
electricity
guide
listened
private
slippery

List 3
accept
believe
crocodile
employ
harbour
lonely
produce
spaghetti

List 4
abuse
boundary
crouch
endangered
headache
machine
prompt
student

List 5
accident
broadcast
cursor
energy
height
magazine
properly
style

List 6
account
broadband
custom
enormous
helicopter
measurement
punctual
successful

List 7
active
busiest
daily
enough
hiccups
meddle
punishment
support

List 8
addiction
capital
dairy
envelope
history
mention
pyjamas
surround

List 9
addition
careful
dangerous
error
hopeful
mobile
quality
Tasmania

List 10
advance
caterpillar
debt
examine
hurriedly
mosquito
quarter
thieves

List 11
advantage
cement
decide
example
hurrying
nation
really
tongue

List 12
advice
centre
decorate
excitement
husband
nearly
reason
tough

List 13
all right
cereal
exercise
ignorant
neither
receive
towel
youth

List 14
although
chemist
defuse
explain
improve
nineteen
referee
trial

List 15
amusement
chief
delight
extinct
inflation
ninety
refrigerator
trousers

List 16
ancient
chocolate
demand
famous
injury
who's
regular
truly

List 17
angle
choir
dense
fashion
interesting
nuclear
remembered
tunnel

List 18
annoy
circus
depend
fatal
nutrients
repair
season
type

List 19
anxious
citizen
describe
favourite
interval
obedient
replies
tyre

List 20
approach
clothing
destroy
fifth
introduce
obstacle
rescue
umbrella

List 21
approve
coarse
detain
flavour
invention
occurred
sandwich
uniform

List 22
argue
collect
dictionary
forbidden
invisibility
ordinary
sauce
unknown

List 23
arrange
comfort
digestion
fortunately
it's
oxygen
scraped
usually

List 24
article
command
difference
fortune
jealous
pastime
scraped
valleys

List 25
athletics
commence
disappear
fourteen
juice
wriggle
versatile
yoghurt

List 26
author
common
discussed
friendship
knit
pause
service
victory

List 27
autumn
compare
domestic
frightened
knowledge
phrase
shield
violent

List 28
available
complete
drawer
furnish
labelled
plough
shoulder
visitor

List 29
balance
concern
drowned
glitter
lasagna
position
shuffle
wealth

List 30
balloon
connect
easiest
glorious
lawn
prepare
signal
welcome

List 31
bandage
consider
easily
good-bye
liberty
women
silence
wharves

List 32
barbecue
consist
effect
grammar
library
previous
sincerely
whom

Answers Homework Tonight 5

UNIT 1 — page 8

Reading
1. remember
2. agreed
3. called
4. wondered
5. nagged
6. Take
7. could be
8. rang
9. wanted
10. worked
11. told
12. stuck
13. glared
14. hate

Q: Nikki wouldn't stay at the library.

Spelling: phone, kitchen, aboard, lightning

English
1. woman
2. wombat
3. computer
4. love
5. the road
6. a table

UNIT 1 — page 9

Maths Knowledge and Skills
1. 486
2. 34
3. sphere
4. 50 or tens
5. 53
6. (rectangle)
7. (prism)
8. 207
9. 851
10. cylinder

Space Geometry – 2D Shapes
hexagon, trapezium, rhombus, octagon

Number
1. 10 503
2. 122
3. 3199
4. 231

Research
1. termites
2. ladybird
3. beetle
4. queen bee
5. lice
6. ant
7. cricket

UNIT 2 — page 10

Reading
1. Hundreds of years ago
2. in Europe
3. in tiny, frail ships
4. on sandbanks
5. on sunken reefs
6. for days
7. in strange lands
8. into the depths

Q: **Real:** accidents, diseases, no wind, fierce storms
Imaginary: monsters, giants, sea serpents

Spelling: violent, monsters, beginner, guide

English
1. an
2. an
3. a
4. a
5. a
6. an
7. a
8. a
9. a
10. a
11. an
12. a

UNIT 2 — page 11

Maths Knowledge and Skills
1. 31
2. 1,2,4,8,16
3. a) pentagon b) parallelogram
4. 5L 750 mL
5. 227
6. 1L 500 mL
7. circle
8. $7
9. (a) (clock) (b) (clock)
10. 4

Numeration
1. 24, 96, 192
2. 80, 20, 10
3. 10, 15, 17$\frac{1}{2}$
4. D16, E20, F24, G28
5. 11,422
6. 31,358
7. 43,001
8. 22,995
9. Thousand
10. tens of thousands
11. 1 or units
12. hundreds

Number
1. 7,175
2. 1360
3. 87.5
4. 138.7

Research
1. i) Guard Security ii) Police Station
2. i) Telstra ii) Digital Phones
3. i) The Sports Centre ii) Civic Theatre
4. i) Jo's Suits ii) Charlestown Square
5. i) Charlestown Buses ii) Bob's Bikes
6. i) Fixem Medical Centre
   ii) Base Hospital
1. carrying of fresh water
2. a means of shelter
3. rainfall to help rice grow
4. regular supply of services
5. warmth

UNIT 3 — page 12

Reading
1. containing
2. disaster
3. structure
4. particular
5. carefully
6. visual
7. inoperable
8. hostile
9. acknowledged

Q1: To destroy the space craft.
Q2: troubles in space

Spelling: facility, option, produce

English
1. that
2. you, me
3. Who
4. I, whose

UNIT 3 — page 13

Maths Knowledge and Skills
1. fifty-seven
2. 365
3. 39
4. (a) $\frac{70}{100}$ (b) $\frac{369}{100}$
5. 38°
6. 37°
7. 44
8. 9
9. 28
10. True

Number– Rounding Off
1. 1000 1200 1230 1234
2. 10,000 9900 9860 9862
3. 6000 6200 6250 6249
4. 1000 1000 1050 1045
5. 37°C
6. 5°C
7. 50°C
8. 100°C

Number
1. 82,374
2. 53.6
3. 272.4
4. 908

Research
Spacecraft: escaping Earth's atmosphere, re-entering Earth's atmosphere
Flightcrew: being weightless in space, being confined to a small area
Ground Control: controlling the spacecraft, talking to the spacecraft
Equipment: electrical power breakdown, communication equipment out of range
(Answers may vary)

UNIT 4 — page 14

Reading
1. 9.16 a.m.
2. 39 minutes
3. 8.48 train, 12 minutes late
4. It doesn't stop at Watson Hall.
5. Catch the 8.14 air-conditioned train.
6. To know exactly what time trains leave and not to waste time waiting.

Spelling: missed, holidays, boundary, student

English
1. can't, sense, books
2. My, they're, too
3. doesn't, know, do
4. exercises, is, than
5. these or those, puzzles, easily

UNIT 4 — page 15

Maths Knowledge and Skills
1. Fourteen thousand, four hundred and seventy nine
2. 44
3. 52
4. 60c
5. 43,871
6. 75
7. 346,000
8. 29, 31
9. 180°
10. 360km

Measurement – Time
1. 12.30, 12.45, 1.15
2. 1.30, 2.00, 2.15, 2.45
3. 3.00, 3.30, 3.45, 4.00
4. putting out roots, growing a strong stalk, bursting into flower, dropping seeds

Number
1. 61 786
2. 73.57
3. 3409
4. 120

Research
1. (a) 171; (b) 146; (c) 53, 327; (d) 192, 291, 301; (e) 151, 314
2. (a) Bluefins; (b) Giant crocodiles; (c) Catfish
3. 96, 208, 102, 128, 30, 79, 218, 267
4. Various answers: two half pages, more pictures, more information, topic seen as more important by the author

UNIT 5 — page 16

Reading
1. surf
2. do
3. sea
4. good
5. for
6. swim
7. warmer
8. southern
9. activities
10. warm
11. long
12. whales
13. see
14. clear
15. long
16. one

Q1: Some countries have agreed to stop killing them.
Q2: whale watching requires patience, whales care for their young

73

Answers Homework Tonight 5

Spelling: massive, binoculars, magazine, style

English
1. mine   2. yours   3. its
4. his   5. her
6. ours (other answers possible)

UNIT 5 — page 17

Maths Knowledge and Skills
1. 45 841
2. 60 000 + 5000 + 800 + 30 + 5
3. 98 762   4. 54
5. True   6. 8
7. 1, 2, 4, 5, 10, 20   8. $14.25
9. 8   10. 2:18

Space Geometry – Position
1. A, Q   4. D, R   7. G, N
2. B, O   5. E, P   8. H, V
3. C, S   6. F, T   9. I, V

Number
1. 5999   2. 2222
3. 397.6   4. 151

Research
Features: 1. blowhole; **2.** eye; **3.** baleen; **4.** humped back; **5.** small back fin; **6.** flipper
Communicate: 1. vocal; **2.** flaps; **3.** blowhole; **4.** clicks; **5.** songs; **6.** pitched; **7.** whales; **8.** hear; **9.** waves; **10.** objects

UNIT 6 — page 18

Reading
1. which   9. salt
2. island   10. decided
3. Sea   11. feeling
4. beside   12. through
5. whether   13. envious
6. wear   14. decision
7. different 15. Saturday
8. sandals   16. too

Q1: It was Saturday and he didn't have to go to school.
Q2: Love being bare-footed; sand is moist
Spelling: a, a, g, r, o, p, c, s

English
1. Gum Tree English   2. I
3. The Australian Opals   4. anyone

UNIT 6 — page 19

Maths Knowledge and Skills
1. 94,735; 18,563; 14,925; 9572
2. 130   3. 12,423
4. 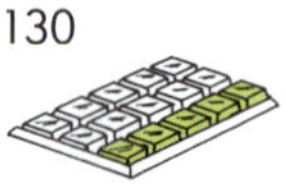   5. 24
6. 6th April
7. $\frac{57}{100}$ 8. 54
9. 16
10. Two hundred and forty-eight

Measurement – Area
a = 10 cm²   b = 19 cm²

Number
1. 43 015   2. 18002
3. 12075   4. 431

Research
R O C K – C R A B J S
M R O W E L T S I R B
A E S E A – H O R S E
X P E R I W I N K L E
S E A – A N E M O N E
S A S P I P I P Y N M
S E A – U R C H I N L
R C M A B E L K C O C

Shells: cockle, periwinkle, pipi
Active and Mobile: sea-horse, rock crab, bristle worm
Attached to rock: sea urchin, sea anemone

UNIT 7 — page 20

Reading
1. F   2. T   3. T
4. F   5. F   6. T
7. F   8. T

Spelling: wonder, system, wrench, imagination, busiest

English
1. talks   2. to fill
3. To think   4. wrote
5. writes   6. to empty

UNIT 7 — page 21

Maths Knowledge and Skills
1. 160   2. 287
3. 0.47   4. 8
5. 25   6. 3
7. 35 cm   8. 100 cm
9. False
10. One thousand two hundred and eighty-five

Measurement – Time
1.  2:45   2.  8:22   3.  9:46
4. 4hr 5min   5. 1hr 38 min

Number
1. 76.65   2. 162.9
3. 321.3   4. 318

Research
1. air, warmth, water and light
2. four sauces
3. cooking oil   4. cotton wool
5. seeds
6. Moisten   7. dry
8. refrigerator
9. cover the seeds with cooking oil

UNIT 8 — page 22

Reading
1. (b)   2. (a)
3. (c)   4. (b)

Spelling: furious, performance, capitol, history, surround

English
1. small   2. yellow   3. white
4. spicy   5. interesting   6. miniature
7. freezing

UNIT 8 — page 23

Maths Knowledge and Skills
1. 500 + 60 + 2   2. 8L 893 mL
3. 
4. $2.30   5. 800
6. 23   7. 4
8. 2L 835 mL   9. 39c
10. 479

Number – Fractions and Decimals
1. 45; 67; 39; 75
2. 0.45; 0.67; 0.39; 0.75
3. $\frac{45}{100}$; $\frac{67}{100}$; $\frac{39}{100}$; $\frac{75}{100}$
4. 45%; 67%; 39%; 75%
5. (a) 0.56 (b) 0.73
6. (a) 0.21 (b) 0.34
7. (a) 0.57 (b) 0.36

Number
1. 173.37   2. 518.51
3. 544   4. 36 r6

Research
Tick: 1, 3, 4, 6, 7, 8
9. Various answers, e.g. (avoid accidents and loss of life)
10. Various answers   11. Various answers

UNIT 9 — page 24

Reading
1. Parent/Teacher
2. Evans St, Park Road, Church Street, Elizabeth Street, Weldon Street, Railway Street
3. Car park
4. Royce Street, Main Road, High Street
5. High Street, Taylor Ave
6. Winning

Spelling: colleges, intersection, dangerous, Zealand

English
1. shouldn't they   5. are, sweet
2. His, Rocky   6. Tammy's, PE
3. Marquez, gave   7. four, cage
4. Do, ?   8. I'll, off

UNIT 9 — page 25

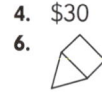

Maths Knowledge and Skills
1. 54   2. 29 m
3. 700 + 60 + 3   4. $30
5. 27,792   6.
7. square pyramid
8. 13 096; 13 690; 13 906
9. 33   10. 1.23

Space and Geometry – Distance
1. 116 km   2. 124 km or 173 km
3. 181 km   4. 313 km

Number
1. 453 502   2. 52990
3. $518.67   4. 133

Answers Homework Tonight 5

Research
New Zealand's two main islands, North Island and South Island, are separated by Cook Strait. Two-thirds of New Zealand's population lives on the North Island. Stewart Island is at the southern tip of the South Island.
1. Auckland
2. Rotorua
3. Wellington
4. Christchurch
5. Mount Cook
6. Milford Sound
7. Stewart Island

UNIT 10 — page 26

Reading
1. world
2. something
3. birds
4. it
5. too
6. water
7. hard
8. pleasant
9. Great
10. coral
11. named
12. years
13. new
14. decide

Q1: Features influencing the naming of oceans and seas.
Q2: Various answers

Spelling: poisonous, decide, debt, thieves

English
1. quickly
2. yesterday
3. here
4. deeply
5. carefully
6. twice
(Answers may vary)

UNIT 10 — page 27

Maths Knowledge and Skills
1. 
2. 61
3. three
4. 68
5. 12
6. 52
7. 100 g
8. 6
9. $\frac{72}{100}$
10. 20th May

Space and Geometry – 3D Shapes
1. 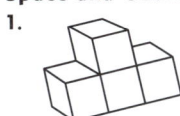
2. 11
3. 17
4. 25
5. 31

Number
1. 112,008
2. 47.9
3. 3674
4. 64 r1

Research – Oceans
1. Indian
2. Timor
3. Arctic
4. China Sea
5. Pacific
6. Tasman Sea
7. Antarctic
8. Atlantic

Question: Mostly the Moon's gravity.

UNIT 11 — page 28

Reading
1. fusses
2. hardly
3. leaking
4. possible
5. knows
6. really
7. finish
8. repairing

Q: Wanted to prove his independence (various answers)

Spelling: i, s, e, c, e

English
1. along
2. Beside
3. Underneath
4. between

UNIT 11 — page 29

Maths Knowledge and Skills
1. 8
2. 8
3. D2
4. B5
5. 15
6. 60c
7. 500 + 7
8. 44
9. 6, 12, 18, 24, 30, 42
10. $365

Space and Geometry – 2D Space
1. trapezium, 2, 2, 1
2. triangle, 0, 0, 3
3. hexagon, 6, 3, 6
4. pentagon, 5, 0, 5
5. rhombus, 2, 2, 0

Number
1. 103,941
2. 7875
3. 1.019
4. 153

Research
1. mechanic
2. doctor
3. engineer
4. choreographer
5. detective
6. chauffeur
7. chef
8. photographer
9. nurse
10. model
11. cleaner
12. programmer

UNIT 12 — page 30

Reading
The correct statements are: 2, 5, 6, 7, 8

Spelling: through, suitable, centre, nearly

English
1. yet
2. and
3. but
4. or

UNIT 12 — page 31

Maths Knowledge and Skills
1. 4
2. 55 years
3. 0°C
4. 50g
5. 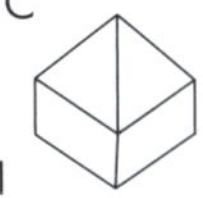
6. 22
7. 91
8. $\frac{2}{3}$
9. 16
10. $50

Measurement – Area
1. 600
2. 44
3. 2
4. 60
5. 10
6. 4
7. 6
8. 260

Number
1. 19,442
2. 3.301
3. 50.68
4. 1.41

Research – Butterfly
1. 10,000
2. day
3. four
4. tiny scales
5. overlapping
6. a mate
7. camouflage
8. a few weeks

UNIT 13 — page 32

Reading
1. (a) The Broncos and The Conquerers
   (b) The Bombers and The Northerners
   (c) The Reds and The Sharks
   (d) The Tigers and The Raiders
2. The Lions
3. Powerhouse Stadium
4. $7,500
5. The Reds, The Broncos, The Bombers, The Raiders and The Warriors
6. Round 9

Spelling: conquerers, Gladiators, Warriors, cereal, ignorant, receive, youth

English
1. new, training
2. taken, one
3. I'm, waiting
4. wonder, team
5. Jack, great

UNIT 13 — page 33

Maths Knowledge and Skills
1. 114
2. 3.56
3. 6
4. obtuse
5. $35.20
6. 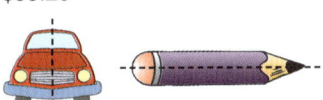
7. 483
8. 11 cm
9. 9 m
10. $\frac{6}{10}$ or 6 tenths

Number – Subtraction
1. H2; T5; U8
2. H8; T0; U0
3. H4; T8; U0
4. 81km
5. 200km
6. 259km
7. 540km

Number
1. 9863
2. 6151
3. 3912
4. 169

Research
1. Spinning tops, Maori
2. Marble arches, score
3. Kite flying, Japanese
4. Answers will vary
5. Answers will vary

UNIT 14 — page 34

Reading
1. (b)
2. (c)
3. (a)
4. (c)
5. dangers of travelling in the 1800s in Australia; problems with transporting gold

Spelling: valuables, snatched, escape, chemist, improve, trial

English
1. pin-up
2. twenty-four
3. brother-in-law
4. pro-active
5. well-liked
6. show-off
7. pre-1994
8. ex-teacher

75

Answers Homework Tonight 5

UNIT 14 — page 35

Maths Knowledge and Skills
1. 40
2. 375, 390
3. 400
4. 2.30
5. 4
6. $\frac{1}{4}$
7. 1435 yrs
8. 66
9. 8
10. 6

Measurement – Volume
1. 76 cm²
2. 146 cm²
3. cm³
4. mL
5. cm²
6. km

Number
1. 622
2. 3.71
3. 21 105
4. 840r7

Research
1. Newcastle
2. Moreton Bay
3. Port Macquarie
4. Sydney
5. Hobart

1. bush robbers and later, bushrangers
2. and only 600 police to catch them
3. guns, horses or proper training
4. flogged with the cat-o-nine tails
5. on farms or roads and escape was easy

UNIT 15 — page 36

Reading
The sentences which do not belong are:
Forbes is a town in New South Wales.
Neville Hopper has dark brown hair.
1. Canowindra
2. Three days
3. Twenty-three
4. Mail coaches, pastoral stations, whole towns
5. In a shoot-out with police, hit by thirty bullets

Spelling: Whole, cruel, bushrangers

English
boxes; ladies; glasses; sheep; shots; oxen; potatoes; wolves; teeth; women; men; heroes; pianos; cupsful; flies; reefs; calves; children.

UNIT 15 — page 37

Maths Knowledge and Skills
1. 144
2. 3
3. 25
4. $9.38
5. 441g
6. 7m 87cm
7. $\frac{89}{100}$
8. 36%
9. Two hundred and sixty-nine dollars and thirty-three cents
10.

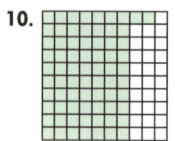

Data – Temperature

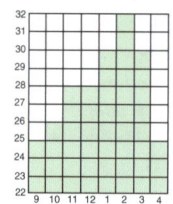

Number
1. 14,1639
2. 38.3
3. 30,060
4. 666 r3

Research
1. smouldering
2. scald
3. extinguisher
4. superficial
5. dressing

UNIT 16 — page 38

Reading
1. Wonder girl, Dolphin Tales, The Rats of Numph, That's Excitement
2. TAS, Everything goes, That's Excitement
3. Repeat
4. Global, Early News
5. Local Round-up
6. Dolphin Tales, Wonderful World
7. Various answers

Spelling: c, u, i, o, u, g, u

English
1. Uncle Paul
2. I appreciated
3. . knew
4. blades The
5. Pretty birthday
6. but.
7. , Natalie

UNIT 16 — page 39

Maths Knowledge and Skills
1. 1
2. 22
3. 180
4. 98
5. 180
6. False
7. 16
8.
9. $2.00
10. 34 minutes

Number – Multiplication
1. 368 × 8 = 2944
2. $2769 × 7 = $19,383
3. 35 × 5 = 175 × 8 = 1400

Number
1. 197 096
2. $24.80
3. $586.96
4. $1.84

Research
1. John Logie Baird
2. Aust 1956 NZ 1960
3. Aust 1975 NZ 1973
4. power zoom
5. microphone
6. zoom lens
7. view finder
8. activating dial
9. video cassette
10. various answers

UNIT 17 — page 40

Reading
1. False
2. True
3. False
4. False
5. True
6. True
7. True
8. False

Spelling: streams, greenhouse, absorb, exhaust, choir, fashion, nuclear, tunnel

English
1. Who
2. This
3. Whose
4. What
5. These
6. whom

UNIT 17 — page 41

Maths Knowledge and Skills
1. 168
2. 0.7
3. 9 months
4. $15.27
5. 78 346; 86 345; 87 456
6. 5400
7. $\frac{1}{2}$
8. 33
9. 312
10. 59 638

Measurement – Mass
1. 180 units
2. 108 units
3. 108 units
4. 72 units

Number
1. 24 042
2. 40.14
3. 26.605
4. 123r4

Research
1. United Kingdom
2. Australia
3. Russia
4. Alaska
5. South Africa
6. Japan
7. Norway
8. United States

UNIT 18 — page 42

Reading
The correct sentences are: 2, 2
Q: Various including: cause choking; cause sore eyes; cannot see to escape etc

Spelling: moment, towels, fatal, season

English
1. Skipping
2. Talking
3. Sailing
4. Running
5. Sneezing
6. Playing

UNIT 18 — page 43

Maths Knowledge and Skills
1. 55
2. 6
3. 92
4. 24 cm²
5. $300
6. 30
7. 14
8. 3
9. 73
10. 110

Answers Homework Tonight 5

Measurement – Time
1.  [clock] 2.  [clock] 3.  [clock] 4.  [clock]
5. 11.45 am   6. 9.00 am

Number
1. 28 608   2. 38.89
3. $6 384   4. 55 r6

Research
1. sun overhead
2. atmosphere
3. scattered blue light
4. sun low in the sky
5. scattered red light
6. Earth   7. Person
8. shines   9. thickness
10. sky   11. orange
12. light   13. scattered

UNIT 19 — page 44

Reading
1. Melt butter in the frypan
2. When melted stir in marshmallows
3. Continue stirring until they are melted
4. Stir in rice bubbles to make stiff mixture
5. Turn off frypan
6. Tear off 30 cm sq of aluminium foil
7. Scoop out mixture to shape into segments
8. Put butter on fingers to mould shape
9. Add pipe cleaner lengths for legs
10. Add sweets for eyes, etc.
11. Avoid burns from hot equipment
12. (Various answers, e.g. burnt mixture needs a lower heat)

Spelling: e, n, x, c, z, a, e, y

English
1. printer, clear   2. my, vivid
3. requires, care
4. lawnmower, racket

UNIT 19 — page 45

Maths Knowledge and Skills
1. 1 500 000   2. sphere
3. 1982   4. 88 cm^2
5. obtuse   6. 1 804
7. 75   8. axis of symmetry
9. 50c   10. 28°C

Working Mathematically – Number Crossword
[crossword grid]

Research
1. Cut and grate carrot
2. Mix the mince, carrot and egg with wooden spoon
3. Heat frypan with some oil
4. Shape mixture into balls and put into frypan
5. Turn meat balls to cook on each side
6. Remove from frypan, drain and serve

UNIT 20 — page 46

Reading
1. loves   7. reasonable
2. really   8. guess
3. phone   9. they're
4. hard   10. simply
5. is   11. pay
6. hour   12. mobile

Q: parent/teacher
Spelling: umbrella, rescue, clothing

English
1. prince   7. steer
2. master   8. monk
3. brave   9. stallion
4. bull   10. hero
5. sultan   11. giant
6. sorcerer   12. heir

UNIT 20 — page 47

Maths Knowledge and Skills
1. $5.00   2. 3500
3. $9   4. [triangle]
5. 43
6. 80 cm   7. 100
8. 8 kg   9. 1408
10. 10 m

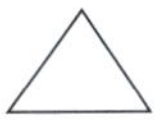

Number – Fractions
1. 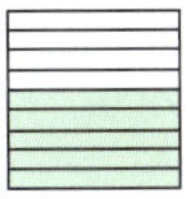 [diagram]   2. 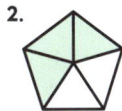 [diagram]   3. 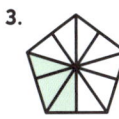 [diagram]
4. One full bucket and one $\frac{2}{5}$ full.
5. One full box and one $\frac{3}{8}$ full

Number
1. 203 472   2. 2 424
3. 544 224   4. 6

Research
1. electricity   5. Satellites
2. tele, phone   6. Mobile
3. microwave   7. magnets
4. facsimile

Big Question: Various answers

UNIT 21 — page 48

Reading
1. miniature   7. completely
2. each   8. jump
3. constant   9. brisk
4. big   10. gently
5. tell   11. magazine
6. describe   12. flank

Spelling: gallop, imagination, flavour, uniform

English
1. nothing to do   2. short of money
3. useless   4. in trouble
5. an ordinary person

UNIT 21 — page 49

Maths Knowledge and Skills
1. $13.50   2. 11.00 a.m.
3. 4   4. 60 cm^3
5. 11, 13, 17, 19   6. 4500
7. 160 cm^3 8. 29 cm
9. 144

Number – Fractions
1. $9.15   2. $13.50
3. $475   4. $4.50
5. $3.75   6. $1.93

Number
1. 37 362   2. 102
3. 7 425   4. 241

Research
Carriage horse: quiet nature; able to pull loads
Race horse: bred and trained to race; can cost a lot of money
Stock horse: help round up cattle; can turn quickly

UNIT 22 — page 50

Reading
1. a young, calfless cow
2. heliograph
3. choose two of the five meanings given
4. can fly straight up and down
5. alphabetical order
6. Shows the first word on the page

Spelling: measure, machine, escape, dictionary, forbidden, ordinary

English
1. flower   2. model
3. waves   4. night
5. stew   6. telephone
7. mean   8. hip
9. tool   10. mouse
11. razor   12. muzzle
13. light   14. seeding

UNIT 22 — page 51

Maths Knowledge and Skills
1. 7   2. thermometer
3. 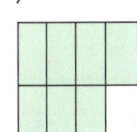 [diagram]
4. 75   5. parallel
6. $56.13   7. 43
8. 260   9. 0.78c
10. 3 and 3

77

Answers Homework Tonight 5

Data – Graphing

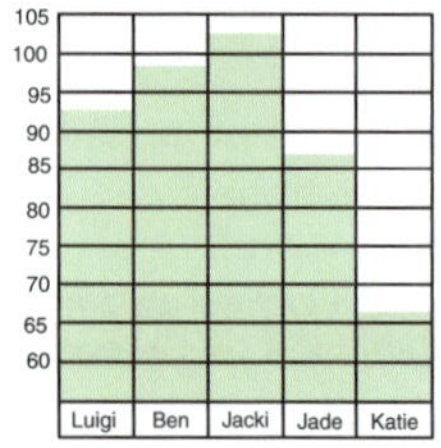

(Bar graph showing values for Luigi, Ben, Jacki, Jade, Katie)

Number
1. 449.89
2. 36.13
3. 1129.2
4. 89.97

Research
1. third
2. Victoria
3. Ireland
4. mountainous
5. plains
6. Bass Strait
7. Devonport
8. Launceston
9. Queenstown
10. Hobart
11. midland areas
12. west coast areas
13. northern areas
14. southern areas

UNIT 23 — page 52

Reading
1. F
2. F
3. F
4. T
5. F
6. T

Spelling: terror, e-mails, regular, arrange, usually

English
1. mouse
2. happiness
3. leg
4. painting
5. pork
6. Sun
7. wash
8. Internet

UNIT 23 — page 53

Maths Knowledge and Skills
1. 444
2. 821
3. 36
4. 9
5. Parent/Teacher
6. 2 000 000
7. 91
8. 20
9. 4
10. 500

Space and Geometry – 3D Space
1. 1, 0, 1, No
2. 12, 8, 0, No
3. 2, 0, 1, No
4. 0, 0, 1, Yes

Nets — Square Pyramid

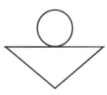

Number
1. 306 770
2. 66.59
3. 279.2
4. 45

Research
1. computers help big planes fly;
2. computers make learning fun;
3. shop without carrying money;
4. computers help organise information;
5. computers help cars run smoothly;
6. chat with friends on the internet.

UNIT 24 — page 54

Reading
1. O
2. F
3. F
4. O
5. F
6. O
7. F
8. O
9. F
10. O
11. F
12. F
13. F
14. O
15. F

Spelling: bananas, chocolate, programs, valleys

English
1. money
2. water
3. sword
4. wine
5. drink
6. tea
7. papers
8. valuables
9. flowers
10. clothes
11. potatoes
12. petrol

UNIT 24 — page 55

Maths Knowledge and Skills
1. $35.25
2. 8
3. 1
4. 5670g
5. (circle diagram)
6. $8.80
7. 247 000
8. 250 000
9. No
10. 18 cm

Number – Division
1. 3152 r1
2. 1425 r2
3. 1272 r2
4. 986 r4
5. 632 r5
6. 277 r3
7. 648
8. 748

Number
1. 131 098
2. 19 894
3. 1 113
4. 1854

Research
1. exposed
2. quarrying
3. reveal
4. uncover
5. skeleton
6. rock
7. value
8. cleaned
9. tools
10. clinging
11. air
12. jigsaw

UNIT 25 — page 56

Reading

The sentences which don't belong are:
Para. 1. Clean your bike regularly.
Para. 2. Some people like surfing and others prefer walking.
1. Yes
2. Difficulty stopping
3. Lights, reflectors
4. Cause an accident
5. Various answers

Spelling: knowledge, conditions, bicycle, obey, fourteen

English
1. self
2. selves
3. self
4. self or selves
5. selves
6. self
7. self
8. self
9. selves

UNIT 25 — page 57

Maths Knowledge and Skills
1. 46%
2. $3.40
3. 139
4. $19.50
5. Nine thousand, eight hundred and thirty-five
6. 180
7. $\frac{4}{10}$
8. True
9. 17
10. 700

Data Co-ordinates
1. Palms
2. Windy
3. Brunker
4. Aura
5. Rio
6. Yukon
7. The Cape
8. Lakes
9. Temora
10. Hidden Bay

Number
1. 198 098
2. 427
3. 596
4. 40

Research
1. (Various) bark, clay, chewed stick
2. (Various) animals, people, Dreamtime, spirits
3. (Various) carving, tattoos, sculpture

UNIT 26 — page 58

Reading
1. National Direct Dialled
2. $2.27
3. 13th Feb, 10.29 p.m. to Clinton for 23.08 min, cost $4.19

Spelling: Brisbane, Adelaide, equipment, payment, discussed, service

English
Adjectives: shy, worried, fearful

UNIT 26 — page 59

Maths Knowledge and Skills
1. 1000
2. (rectangular prism)
3. 4 m
4. 200 kg
5. 40
6. 5
7. obtuse
8. 67c
9. $\frac{1}{100}$
10. eighteen thousand, nine hundred and three

Value for Money
1. 8.80 × 10
   88.00 - 55.00 = $33
2. 1.20 × 20
   24.00 - 18.50 = $5.50

Number
1. 80 016
2. 689
3. $240.79
4. 947r6

Research
Animal: cougar; sloth; lemur; eland; lynx; mongoose.
Vegetable: aniseed; artichoke; yam; marrow; bok choy.
Mineral: quartz; calcite; gypsum; diamond; graphite.
Insect: bee; ant; mosquito
Bird: rosella; kiwi; eagle
Fish: trout; cod; bream

Answers Homework Tonight 5

UNIT 27 — page 60

Reading
1. wink at you
2. special blue coloured glasses
3. has a problem with too much light
4. screaming out
5. I'm losing my place
6. because of my very special third

Question: Some of the light from the page hurt her eyes.

Spelling: plastic, statement, information, domestic, violent

English
1. past
2. future
3. past
4. present
5. future
6. present

UNIT 27 — page 61

Maths Knowledge and Skills
1. 14°C
2. 10
3. 91
4. 180°
5. (clocks)
6. $1.50
7. $8\frac{4}{5}$
8. 6
9. 63
10. 20;200; 20,202; 22 020; 22,220

Measurement – Mass
1. 1600 g; 1 kg 600 g; 1.6 kg
2. 4150 g; 4 kg 150g; 4.15 kg
3. 5920 g; 5 kg 920 g; 5.92 kg
4. 2800 g; 2 kg 800 g; 2.8 kg
5. 6125 g; 6 kg 125 g; 6.125 kg
6. 70 g
7. 230 g
8. 1400 g
9. 3.67 kg

Number
1. 775 113
2. 468.90
3. 312
4. 8100 r1

Research
1. Muscle
2. Cornea
3. Fluid
4. Retina
5. Lens
6. Iris
7. Blood supply
8. Optic nerve
9. Sclera
10. An eye doctor
11. It provides plastic lenses for cataract patients in under-privileged communities.

UNIT 28 — page 62

Reading
1. 84 kilometres
2. Muddy Road, F106 Freeway, Clay Road, Maria Drive, Great Eastern Road, Little Bite Road
3. 1.3 kilometres
4. Educational Activities
5. The Mosquito Band performs
6. $132.50
7. Yes

Spelling: mosquito, property, admission, adults, kilometres

English
"Are we all going to visit Newcastle for the Match of the Day between Newcastle Knights and Auckland Warriors?" asked Kent excitedly.
"You bet!" replied Maui. "We'll give them a game to remember!"

UNIT 28 — page 63

Maths Knowledge and Skills
1. one century
2. 300 thousand
3. 19, 23, 29
4. 57
5. 76
6. 20
7. 91
8. 13
9. (cross shape)
10. 6

Space Geometry – Space
1. (grid)
2. (grid)

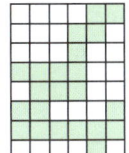

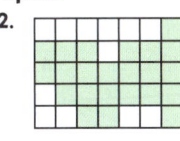

Number
1. $1353.52
2. 969
3. 324
4. $1\frac{1}{4}$

Research
1. True
2. False
3. True
4. False
5. False

1. legs
2. balancing legs
3. sucking tube
4. larva
5. breathing tube
6. pupa

Question: Two weeks.

UNIT 29 — page 64

Reading
1. No, Alison is
2. Alison
3. Fiji
4. By plane
5. New Zealand
6. Four
7. Go to an extinct volcano
8. Yes, because she likes the markets
9. Yes, because she talks about the pool, the beach, an extinct volcano and the markets
10. Lewisville, NSW

Spelling: concern, glorious, extinct, holiday

English
1. gathered overhead
2. threaded the needle carefully
3. make life hard for children
4. are seldom seen

UNIT 29 — page 65

Maths Knowledge and Skills
1. 45°
2. 13
3. thirty four thousand, six hundred and ninety
4. 6.467 kg
5. two points
6. 56%
7. 9th, 12th, 23rd
8. protractor
9. (ellipse)
10. (clock)

Area
A = 3 x 5 = 15cm²
B = 3 x 3 = 9cm²
C = 2 x 5 = 10cm²
Total = 34cm²

Number
1. 246.91
2. $30.11
3. 377.60
4. 334

Research
1. 1642 Abel tasman sighted New Zealand – blue
2. 1815 Road over the Blue Mountains – green
3. 1840 Treaty of Waitangi – blue
4. 1854 Eureka Stockade battle – green
5. 1860 First Taranaki War – blue
6. 1880 Ned Kelly, the bushranger hanged – green
7. 1882 **Dunedin** transported frozen meat to England – blue
8. 1901 Federation of Australian states – green

UNIT 30 — page 66

Reading
1. Hometown, Novel East, Charlesville, East Miles, Kathay
2. $1267.34
3. At Ellersley's Sales at Charlesville for $230 and Lambs Timber at Hometown for $79
4. $0.50
5. The Bank
6. $2150.54

Spelling: electric, foundation, received, financial, balloon, glorious

English
Teacher/Parent
Answers will vary.

UNIT 30 — page 67

Maths Knowledge and Skills
1. (half-shaded circle)
2. 50%
3. 1000 years
4. $19.60
5. rectangular prism
6. 6 hundredths
7. 450 mm
8. 1000
9. 5
10. 7.4 m

Data – Graphs

Ford $8000	$ $ $ $ $ $ $ $
Toyota $10,000	$ $ $ $ $ $ $ $ $ $
Holden $5000	$ $ $ $ $
Nissan $7000	$ $ $ $ $ $ $
4WD $9000	$ $ $ $ $ $ $ $ $
Trucks $6000	$ $ $ $ $ $
Subaru $5000	$ $ $ $ $

Number
1. 89 209
2. $25.25
3. $1488.00
4. 1012 r6

Answers Homework Tonight 5

Research
1. shells, salt, stones
2. gold
3. penny
4. legal tender
5. ingots
6. government
7. weight

UNIT 31 — page 68

Reading
The correct sequences are:
1. G, D, F, E, A, C, H, B
2. C, F, A, E, G, H, B, D

Spelling: advice, bicycle, defective, ignored, luckily, permission

English
1. threw, sitting
2. gave, complete
3. dropped, raced
4. be, kicked

UNIT 31 — page 69

Maths Knowledge and Skills
1. 35
2. rectangular prism
3. 478
4. sphere
5. False
6. 0635
7. Compass rose (N, NE, E, SE, S, SW, W, NW)
8. $32.62
9. 0.26
10. 5.02

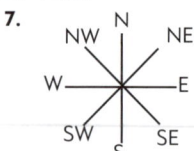

Number – Fractions – Decimals
1. 77; $\frac{77}{100}$; 7T 7H; 0.77; 77%
2. 65; $\frac{65}{100}$; 6T 5H; 0.65; 65%
3. 27; $\frac{27}{100}$; 2T 7H; 0.27; 27%
4. 43; $\frac{43}{100}$; 4T 3H; 0.43; 43%
5. 83; $\frac{83}{100}$; 8T 3H; 0.83; 83%
6. (pentagon diagram)
7. (triangle strip diagram)

Number
1. 342 992
2. 989
3. 1029
4. 306 r3

Research
1. rub together
2. electricity, light and heat
3. 800, two, between

UNIT 32 — page 70

Reading
1. Sydney Harbour, Lake Macquarie, Newcastle coastline, Hawkesbury River, Berowra Waters, Brisbane Water National Park
2. By boat
3. Toilets – too many needed (various answers)
4. Very tall trees, unique vegetation
5. To preserve the environment (various answers)

Spelling: Newcastle, experience, venture, impressive, purchase, necessary

English
1. mum's/terrific
2. strawberry/bread
3. went/pizza

UNIT 32 — page 71

Maths Knowledge and Skills
1. 8.01
2. 21
3. 180 km
4. greater than 180°
5. (triangular prism diagram)
6. 1.9 cm
7. 17, 19, 23, 29
8. $\frac{3}{4}$
9. No
10. $3400

Working Mathematically – Calculator
1. 207
2. 402
3. 89
4. 14.44
5. 118.5
6. 111
7. 3.01; 3.17; 3.25; 3.3; 3.68
8. 0.163; 0.188; 0.199; 0.217; 0.258

Number
1. 500 164
2. $41.63
3. $513.03
4. 110 r3

Research

Across
2. track
4. lake
5. emergency
7. tent

Down
1. pack
3. care
4. light
6. map

80